The War of Canneti

Ankit Roy

ISBN: 9798776862212

DEDICATION

To mum, more than forever.

Contents

A quarante huict degre climaterique
A fin de Cancer ſi grande ſeichereſſe
Poiſſon en mer fleuue lac cuit hectique
Bearn Bigorre par feu ciel en destresse.

At the forty-eighth climacteric degree,
At the end of Cancer very great dryness.
Fish in sea, river, lake boiled hectic,
Bearn, Bigorre distress through fire from the sky.

-Nostradamus Century V, Qua. 98

ACKNOWLEDGMENTS

This book wouldn't have been possible without the support of my father, sister, wife and little Rudrayn who endured my continued absence from their lives until the manuscript was complete.

This book is also the testimony to Author Sweta Samota's excellent skills as a writing coach for budding authors.

I would also thank Author Jerry Jenkins for his masterful editing techniques and for his excellent feedback.

A final note of gratitude to all my friends in the Indian Army whom I pestered with countless questions and they answered.

1 HIGHWAY TO HELL

The drill hammered a thousand kilometres under the ground. Innards of the planet churned out huge mounds of earth that grew bigger and bigger every second. Dirt, mud, chalk and water piled up. Dev looked over his shoulder, through the small glass window. The lift at the entrance of the 'hell hole' was visible to his left. From the control tower, twenty feet high, it looked like a gateway to the underworld. A thick orange pipe marked the way through which the cables dragged down to the checkpoint. Whiff of Smoke raised from the exhausts installed deep inside the hole. The checkpost that housed the control equipment was five kilometers deep inside the crust. The farthest any man had ever gone! He called it the 'hell-hole' for it reminded him of Dante's seven circles of hell. He looked at the entrance and thought about the cool and soothing cabin at the checkpoint. He hated the barren lands and the eerie tranquillity of Russian Siberia. He had an uneasy feeling whenever he did ground duty. Working inside was safe! If something went wrong you would know.

He didn't know what they would do once they reach the threshold of the crust. It could be any minute now. They had been digging for over five years, ever since the war had stopped. For decades, this place was under the snow and now the snow had melted.

All of it!

The earth here was soft. Technicians Steve and Luis were monitoring the circuit today. They were at the checkpoint five kilometres below. That left him alone to endure dead nature. Here he had one responsibility. He had to ensure the safety of the fusion plant. The reactor was a humongous building 280 meters in length and 500 meters wide. It stood atop a hill some 2 miles away, connected with the drill through probes of purest copper and gold. That's what they were drilling for with those expensive equipment. After the Great War, power stations around the world stopped generating electricity. Courtesy effect of a nuclear holocaust. The world council had resolved to drill deep and connect the core to harness its energy. The Earth's core! Even in broad daylight, it sounded absurd. The pressure inside was three thousand times the deepest oceans. The temperature, close to the sun. A fusion chamber attached to a titanium drill to end the world's energy need forever? Sounded like science fiction! Clean energy for millenniums to come. Dev knew this was happening. And he was a part of this project. Although he wasn't a patriotic in the stricter sense of things, he felt proud being an Indian. It validated his identity with the country that would solve the energy need of the entire world. Digging 1300 feet inside the Earth was a monumental task. Then there was the layer of molten lava. Rumours were rife that Steller Green (the corporation that had taken up the project) had spent three times what the last world war had cost. A whooping 86 trillion US dollars (or 62 trillion Indian Rupees, the prime currency after the war). Roughly seventy percent of the world economy. A quantum heat absorber designed by a former CEO of the company protected the drill from the extreme conditions inside the Earth. The device didn't need energy to work. It manipulated the intense heat on a quantum level and dissipated it in the cryogenic drive pedals that propelled it forwards. But this energy was too huge for the probes and sensors on the machine. The manipulation of heat at the atomic level left a rare chance of an atomic collision. It could cascade into a chain reaction, turning the core into a nuclear bomb. To stop this from happening, the drill had a lithium chroniton limiter. An ingenious little device that needed a plasma coolant. He had learnt all this in the labs where the device was first proposed.

He took a deep breath and continued to stare back at the screen.

The machine went deeper and deeper and he kept looking. The green dot blinked every second and went on. It was hours away from the outer core. Their sector would be the first to connect with the core.

Steve and Luis were working inside the tunnel today. Dev had been there last week. This job was not for the weak hearted. Inside the tunnel, it felt like the insides of a giant reptile complete with echoing voice. The stalactites and stalagmites looked like the many teeths of the reptilian monster. Working twelve hours straight inside the hell-hole, hot humid and dark. For some, it was better to risk cancer in the sun than to be inside listening to the the soft whirring of the computer. For Dev, it was heaven. The last checkpoint was five kilometer deep. After this point, the hole was a tiny twenty inch head. It was large enough for the titanium drill to connect the gold and copper tubes to allow heat exchange. They had selected 8 strategic points to drill, spread out over the volcanic belt of the Siberian Kamchatka River. It had over 160 volcanoes, 12 of them still active. He was in one of these 'hell holes'

The radar stopped blinking.

Dev looked up at the screen. The drill had stopped, the meter mark was constant to the decimal and nothing moved.

Amazed, Dev muttered "Did we reach the core?"

He pressed a green button on the console in front of him. A red light started to blink. He then pressed the button next to a grill and yelled, "Steve, Luis?" There was no answer.

He pressed the button again and screamed, "Steve, you in there?"

A soft crackle followed by the voice of Steve echoed. "Go ahead, I'm right here"

"The drill stopped" Dev said.

"I'm detecting an anomalous power spike in the limiter." Steve answered.

"Can you see anything?" Dev knew this was a foolish question.

"Nothing here! Just the dark"

"Why did it stop?" Dev said.

"Luis…" yelled Steve.

There was a scuffling of feet and the voice of Luis echoed. "Hey it's a power failure. Dev be a good boy. Go and check the solar panels."

Dev hated it when Luis called him a good boy. He felt like his little pet. He knew the more he protested, the more Luis will bring it up. He said it was his Irish blood. Dev knew for a fact that it was the stupid in him.

"I'll go check on the panels" he said.

He rushed down the stairs, slid across the long plastic neck and reached the changing room at the bottom. He put over the white suit and helmet, zipped it close and rechecked it in the mirror. He didn't want another bruise on his belly from the sun exposure. They were quite intense here in Siberia. The ozone layer had dissolved. Some places on the mainland were safe, but out here it was intense. He opened the door and walked into a blazing sun. A couple of centuries ago, if you had 'walked into the blazing sun' in January, people would've called you schizophrenic. Not anymore. They were the stuff of period drama novels. He had learned in geography that the winter of the Kamchatka Peninsula had drifted inwards. Dev looked at the carcinogenic Sun and squinted to adjust to the light. This was the fifth time he was going out there. He looked around at the copper ground and spotted the array of solar panels gleaming in the distance. The heat made it look like simmering away in the blue sky. A ten minute walk from where he stood. Not wanting to spend time more than required, he set forth. He was sweating in about half a minute of walking down the field. He kept on! Using vehicles was a crime, ever since petrol and diesel exhausted. He walked through the beige ground. The heat inside the suit made him sweat like a fat pig. He heaved his legs and pushed. 'Just a yard more.' His back burnt with the heat. He was cooking in his own sweat. What a fine stew he would make. He should have bought some water. The thought made him gulp but his parched throat didn't even move. 'A few yards more' he went on. He opened the wicket gate and entered the solar yard. He slumped under one of the panels and reached for the iron structure for support, heaving. He took a deep breath and recovered. He had a job to do. He hauled himself and started to check the wires.

As soon as he turned around, a blinding flash like the sun burned away his vision. He covered his eyes but, even though his thick white suit, he could see the blood vessels of his palms. The corners of his eyes itched and he heard the concrete tower collapse to the ground with a thunder. The heat was now unbearable and he felt like his body dipped in sulphuric acid. He fell to the ground and tried to turn away from the heat and the light. He screamed! A pitiless screech of pain! Then everything went dark.

Dev tried to get up but he couldn't move. His joints ached and it took every ounce of his energy to turn. He couldn't see anything. Then wisp of shapes took form, like dull silhouettes in winter fog. He could make out the backdrop of the Kronotsky point. A ball of grey smoke rose from it and the earth around him shuddered with its might. The control tower was gone. He scratched his eyes to focus but all it did was itch even more. Something must have gone wrong. His vision dimmed further. He couldn't make out the fence of the solar park. He gave a mighty itch to his eyes and jerked his head. He raised his hands in front of him. He knew they were right there but he couldn't see. Darkness engulfed him. What had happened in there! The quantum manipulation could've led to a chain reaction. But the chances of it happening were one in a million. If probability had hit then the system had collapsed on itself. The core must have gone a quantum shift. Packing and unpacking huge amount of energies until there was nothing left to burn. Dev knew there was only one way to stop. The core would collapse into itself and then unpack. Hot molten lava at 4500 degrees collapsing and then erupting in less than a nanosecond. If the calculations of the engineers were correct, it would take exactly 72 hours for it to cascade. The entire 1.8 billion cubic miles of the core would be a nuclear bomb! And seep to a level where it would gain enough energy to make earth collapse on itself. There were 72 Angels of God, he had learned that in school. A voice in his head echoed, 'one hour for each Angel you pray to.'

Dev jerked his head and groped for the radio on his belt. He had to alert the authorities. The message had to go out. Seventy two hours was too less a time for the humans to escape. He put every ounce of his energy to pull out the radio, ripped it from his waistband and pressed the record button. He had kick-started the apocalypse!

2 THUNDERSTRUCK

For the first time in 14 thousand years, geography had changed. Madhav looked a sea gull flying above the submerged turrets of the Bandra-Worli sea link. It dropped into the space in the middle of the bridge. With a spectacular flip, it emerged victorious, clutching a large black fish gleaming in the sun, and sat atop the tower. The rusty, iron pylons looked like the fangs of a dead monster. The grey sea mirrored the black skies above. Madhav skittered under the shade of a skyscraper and rushed towards Marathon Apartments. The shops on the road were boarded up. Broken glass, stray animals and a heap of garbage lay abandoned on the sides. He hurried past them in hopes of having an early dinner. He had a rough day at work and looked forward to the warmth of his rooms. He entered the building and stopped. He took deep breaths and regained his might. Although there was an elevator but there was no power to run it. Slowly, he started the ascent. At the twentieth floor, he pushed open his apartment door and slumped on the couch catching a stitch at his side gasping for breath. Ever since the war, the power supply had been curtailed to five hours a day. For the rest, Solar panels were the only choice. Madhav pushed open a window and looked out at the infinite sea. He had considered moving to a lower level but it was too much work. His company sold batteries and most of the people had fled Mumbai after the flash floods of last year. The sea had already reduced the city to seven separate islands. The islands occasionally connected by the Pydhoine creek during the low tides revealing a sprawling city underneath.

The intercom buzzed and the voice of a kid crackled. "Madhav bhaiya,

food!"
Madhav moved over to the door and answered over the intercom, "You are late Raja. Now you'll have to come up to deliver"
"I'm not late you are early" Raja said.
"Come on! You can watch the television with me"
There was a pause. Raja stood there for a second then said, "I'll be there."
Within ten minutes the kid stood at Madhav's doorway. He held out a worn-out white Tupperware box that locked his supplements for the day.
Madhav rubbed his hands together "What's in there tonight?" he asked.
"Same old. Soybean curry"
Madhav's face fell. "Fifth time in a row. Last month it was mushrooms."
"It's so expensive you could buy gold for a sack of potatoes" Raja said.
He knew Raja was right. Farming and produce were ruined, factories stopped for lack of energy. Humans needed a reset button.
"It's the war. It should never have happened." Raja said.
"You are too young to know. Ever saw these towers in the middle of the ocean? Know what they are? They are the railway lines connecting the islands."
"Those ugly pillars? Bhati told me they were oil rigs"
"Bhati is a fool. And it was a hundred year ago. Anyways, it's not only the war. Its greed."
"Greed for what?"
Madhav knew it was hard to explain. He chewed his food and swallowed it before answering, "All this stuff that we have. All these buildings, vehicles... all this" he rolled his finger around, "came from factories. Factories needed raw material. They dug the earth, burnt coal and expended fuels to cover distances beyond measure. Look what it did to the planet."
"You said we could watch TV" said Raja, uninterested.
"Doesn't it bother you? The rains, the cold, the snow in Mumbai?"
"Bhati says you are a madman. You believe all these conspiracy theories."
Bhati was a fool, "What conspiracy theories?"
"That cars could run on electricity but the petrol companies didn't want them to sell"
Madhav threw up his arms in exasperation. "It's true" he yelled.
He knew for a fact that the vehicle manufacturers had stalled the developments electric cars. It was a huge scandal back in the 3100's. The Motorcade Scandal. Environmental activists, researchers and scientists had taken to the road blaming crony capitalism. A committee was constituted. They came out with their fact. Millions of vehicles had already been produced. Millions of Tonnes of raw material and labour had been paid for. Not selling them would be catastrophic to the world entire. Courts around the world acquitted the manufacturers. Environmentalists cried foul. And the world forgot. Like they forgot the Holocaust.

"You said we could watch TV" Raja pressed on.

He loathed humans. Madhav threw the TV remote at him and said, "Oh here it is."

The seas had been rising for years, but the last century had been different. The Great War in the Middle East was violent on a scale that cannot be thought possible. First it was the inflation. The war effort demanded more and more factory produce. And an even greater labour. Like a carrot on a stick, man produced in hopes of riches. And like the greedy creature he was, he warred on for more oil fields and land. The warring intensified, each side believing God was with them. When fanaticism meets nationalism, nobody but the innocent perish. A quarter of the world's population was killed. Everyone was a martyr. For each side believed they were the saviour. Satan laughed! There was no end to greed. And greed destroyed the very fabric of man's environmental support system. Heavy nuking of the Middle East erased the holy lands forever. A cascade of nukes destroyed the new world. The Earth quaked! The Sun darkened! The Moon turned red!

Raja looked up at Madhav and asked, "Why didn't you leave? You are famous and wealthy."

Wealth didn't matter anymore. Madhav smiled and said, "I wasn't on the list."

The United Nations set up controlled migration to colonize Mars and the Moon. The world council approved and created a list of humans eligible for migration. All the politicians and businessmen of stature had managed to make the list. A inter planetary bank was set up to provide Martian or Lunar land equivalent to their property on Earth. The UN restricted the applications citing limited natural resources. That left the less privileged to survive on their own. Since the governments were the first to flee, scientists and researchers stayed behind to help. Madhav had stayed behind in too.

"I'd like to go" Raja said.

"Where are your parents? Why didn't they take you there?"

"My father died in the war. Mother passed away and I ran away from home."

"Ran away and came here?"

"I didn't know where I was going. A fat guy gave me a lift. But didn't let me get down his van. He made me extract morphine from the poppy fruit. One night he got high as usual and came to me. He was naked and had a knife in his hand. I got scared and flipped the vat of scalding opium water on him and ran away. I slept on a side road under a garbage heap. Bhati found me in the morning and we started to deliver food for money."

"You are brave..." Madhav said.

"I don't like to think about it. I'd leave earth if I could."

He flipped the channel to a tele-shopping network.

Democracy had been overthrown by a glorious people's revolution that ended up destroying half the world. The charismatic leader from the east promised a utopia where there was no poverty, no class distinction and no injustice. Pure equality! His rants in the party meeting always started with the example of the French revolution.

"Blood," he said is a price people should be ready to pay for a glorious uprising! Those in power will always oppose for the fear of losing their privileges. The French revolution, the Russian revolution and the American war of Independence happened at a time India was busy fighting the tyranny of the colonists. The British and the weak and pathetic Indian rulers shut the country from rest of the world. We missed that train! To get away with a weak country, we were given Independence in charity. It was more to the economic death of the colonists, than our revolutionaries. We were blindfolded and made to believe that the struggle of Indian Independence was hard earned. A peaceful movement respected all around the world. All lies!

We call our fighters revolutionary terrorists. We accept dominion. For centuries we endure corruption, treason and terrorism. Not anymore. Comrades, time has come for the people of India to rise."

People, fed up with the corruption in government offices and the inequality of jobs gave him a chance. To tackle global warming, the western world pressurized countries in the Indian subcontinent to stop industrialization. The crisis that followed led to the third world war. When he finally became a dictator, he instigated a strict one party system. He discredited the Geneva Climate Change Protocols and brought about massive industrialization. Wreaking the environment was the least of everyone's concern. When war broke out, hell unleashed.

The rising seas had already divided Pakistan right in the middle. Supreme leader annexed the provinces of Baluchistan and Punjab while the combined forces of Russia and China ate up the rest. United States felt betrayed and joined forces with the Arab countries. Soon Israel joined Russia, India and China against the US and the Arabs. The fundamentalist in Arab opposed the American support. In what is known as the Red November, a series of terror attacks in US made it switch sides and join the Alliance of the East or AE. The AE took one of the bloodiest decisions in the history of humankind. To nuke the Middle East.

A cascade of nuclear attacks and counter attacks heated the earth to boiling point. India pushed it borders into the islands of Norway and Finland (rising seas had wiped out rest of Europe. France and Germany were reduced to islands along with UK, Sweden and Norway). The Great War went on for five years and a quarter of the world's population died. Prices of natural oil and gas went towering and was soon followed by a total ban on fossil fuels. The world plunged, once again, into the Dark Age. Not of ignorance, but of power. Electricity was not anymore a basic necessity.

It wasn't even a luxury.

It was magic.

And just like magic, no one knew how to wield it!

Madhav watched the kid as he immersed himself into this world of myriad information. Most of it to urge them to buy something or the other. Consumerism!

I own a TV too. He did, but to remain updated. For the connect it provided and not for cheap entertainment. This was an older version. Superior products or Ariel, as they were called, were introduced long ago. They took the market by storm. People enjoyed soap opera immersed in the virtual world of the show itself! But he liked the old fashioned screen type. He was not much of a TV addict and used it to play computer games and surf the internet. And he hated the helmets. Raja flicked the channel again. A girl in soft pink skirt danced to a rapid beat of percussions. Raja ogled at the screen open mouthed.

Suddenly, the screen went blank.

"Battery dead! Khallas!" Raja said, rolling the remote away on the floor.

This couldn't be true. He had enough juice in the batteries to run a car. His old fashioned TV was negligible.

The LED blinked green. The screen juddered and a neatly dressed TV anchor came up. The logo of Democracy News! See it to believe it! Flashed on the screen.

"This just in. We have unconfirmed reports that a drilling experiment in the North Eastern Russia may have gone terribly wrong."

The scene changed and a volcano appeared on the screen, spewing and spitting grey smoke in the distance. The sound of chopper blades drowned most of what the reporter said.

It was in a different language. A ribbon with subtitles circled across the screen.

Kronotsky volcano- Steller Green India's clean energy project base.

The chopper went down towards a lake. The screen showed a brown landscape. One end of the field had a rubble of blue and silver mangled into what looked like 'hit by a freight train'. A thin curl of smoke rose from the other end of the land. The camera zoomed out.

"This is once again, a picture of the Kronotsky Volcano"

The screen switched to the studio.

"These are very disturbing images. Obviously something devastating has happened. And again there are unconfirmed reports of a quantum explosion close to the core of the earth."

Madhav leaned closer to the screen. Raja had stood up.

The anchor continued, "Right now we've got Rohit Gandhi -our editor in chief- on the phone.

Rohit what can you tell us about this explosion reported by the Russian media?

"This is Rohit Gandhi. I was talking to our Russian media partner…"

"Rohit we are live! We are On-Air now!"

"Hello?" The voice crackled with static.

"Yes, Rohit. We are live right now. What can you tell us about this explosion in Siberia?"

Locals at the Milkovo village saw a blinding cloud of light, 'as bright as the sun'. This is a conserved eco-region and entry to the nature reserve is restricted. The Russian Government has initiated a search & rescue operation. People felt the Earth shudder like an earthquake. There is panic in the area."

"Rohit, what kind of experiment was it? A dig for more oil, you think?"

"Well, Steller Green hasn't come up with a statement yet. But it is rumoured that a fusion reactor…"

The anchor cut short his editor in chief and the company logo flashed across the screen with its familiar fanfare.

"This just in. An audio transmission has been discovered. One of the employees of Steller Green has released an audio message. The message was sent by a senior scientist working at the control tower directly above the explosion"

A screech of audio like bad reception played for a second. Then there was a deep voice with an Indian accent, "This is senior scientist Dev Patel, assigned section 1 of the Steller Green Clean Energy Foundation. Section one of the core drilling operation has cascaded into a quantum explosion. I repeat, it has caused an explosion kilometres away from the outer core. The entire earth will collapse into the quantum manipulation effect within seventy two hours. The planet must be evacuated! There is no way to stop this!"

The news anchor was back on screen. His poker face gave nothing away.

"Again, you are looking at pictures now. We understand that an experiment to harness the earth's core has exploded into one of the control towers of the Steller Green Clean Energy Foundation. You can see the smoke billowing out of the mine. There are flames out there. At this point, we do not have official injury updates to bring you. We are only now beginning to put together the pieces of this horrible incident. We have Rohit back on phone. Rohit what can you tell us about this incident? Is the audio message correct?"

Rohit's voice echoed from the screen. "I can just tell you, the Russian officials are also telling me that the -- this is clearly a catastrophic accident in their view, and they believe that this might be the last act of humans on the planet.

However, they have very little other information. Obviously, the world energy council will be taking a lead on this, trying to find out what technology was used for these detonations and so on, so very little information.

 "Rohit, we're going to have to cut you off. Prime Minister Vajra is speaking."

3 NO MORE NICE GUY

On and on it went. All the channels played the message of the Indian Prime Minister in synchronisation. Addressing the Earth from his Martian base, The Prime Minister advised everyone to evacuate. He assured that the world governments will provide support and mechanism in every way possible. Then the screen went blank.

Raja turned around to face Madhav and said, "Is it true? 72 hours?"

"No! Not 72!" Madhav did the math. It took twenty minutes for messages from Earth to reach the Martian base. A round of inquiries and investigations, reports and conclusions. Must have taken another ten to twelve hours. Then they must have authorized the broadcast. So now they had somewhere around sixty hours left. Even less.

"What do we do now, bhaiya?"

Raja was speaking slowly, deliberately, as if in denial that anything so horrible could be happening.

A whoosh of a car outside took them by surprise. Madhav hurried over to the window to look. An impenetrable darkness engulfed the outside as usual. He could make out tiny pin pricks of a car headlight in the distance. More engines revved up, the air was rife with action.

Madhav turned around "There's no time! We must leave now."

"And go where?"

"To the evacuation point"

Tears streamed down Raja's eyes. He didn't seem so mature. More like a child lost at a fair.

"There's only one evacuation point in India. And its thirteen hundred kilometres away."

Madhav exclaimed at the exactness of the figure Raja used. But it didn't matter. Nothing mattered.

"That's our only hope"

"But how are we going to go there? Do you have a car with enough batteries?"

They could nick a car. Thousands of them lay abandoned at the dead showroom a few blocks away from his factory.

"How long does it take to reach Sriharikota?" He said more to himself than to Raja. He reached for his communication device and started to type.

"Twenty four hours by road"

Madhav looked up, his face glowing under the luminance of the communication device.

Just then a loud voice echoed from the streets. A crowd had gathered and were yelling at the top of their lungs for people to come out of their house. It was hard to see anything in the darkness. Madhav squinted and saw more and more people swarming in the middle of the road, or what was left of the road.

He turned to face Raja and said, "Let's go. I know what to do.

Madhav was standing in the centre of the crowd. All eyes were on him as he turned on the spot looking at everyone. Some of the faces were familiar. Raja, Bhati- the boy who ran the restaurant, the old woman who always covered her head with a stole and the man who worked opposite Madhav's factory. A soft drizzle fell from the heavens. 'If ever there was a heaven.'

"There are some cars at the Samota car showroom. Let us storm down their doors take away the cars and leave for Sriharikota."

Some cheered with a dull clapping that died away in seconds. Some stared at him.

"What if the cars don't start?" A man said.

"What if they do not allow us to leave?" The ugly old woman said.

"We got to try" said the kid next to Raja,

"We need drivers and only four of us can travel in a car, five at the most." Said Raja.

"Let's go! We cannot waste time" Bhati said.

The crowd pushed and shoved, like a basket of lobsters jostling to get out. Finally, Madhav reached out to Raja and pulled him forward, "Let them go to hell. I'm going." And marched away.

The crowed followed. Madhav looked behind to see the old lady with the headdress was among them.

They reached the showroom in twenty minutes. It was abandoned and Madhav let the crowd do its job.

The crowd pushed harder now, bodies jammed against each other. It had turned into an angry beast. The beast charged down the front doors. The glass shattered and they moved in. Madhav swept inside with them, his feet leaving the floor for a second. Someone crashed the windows. Shards of glass came flying through the air as the crowd pushed itself deeper into the room. There were twelve cars on the second floor. Only one on the first. Soon, people began to struggle to get inside. The first one drove away with three men inside. Another drove away stuffed with three men, a young women and two babies. Those left behind started to panic. The cars took off one by one. People rushed to others and begged to be inside. A tall man got stuck in the car window and dragged along the road stuck to it. Madhav dashed out to help him. The man was lying half way down the road crawling towards the side. It was pitch black with not a star in sight. Madhav pulled the man to his feet and turned. Two more cars zoomed past him. He rushed back to the showroom. The old lady and Raja stood in the middle of the hall with not a car in sight. Everyone had fled.

The injured man limped behind them and groaned. All four were silent.

"Madhav bhaiya!" Raja said, "What do we do now?" His voice echoed inside the empty building.

He looked at them. If these were the last humans left on Earth, it couldn't be the second coming after all.

"I don't know" He answered.

The old woman said, "Is there no other way we can get out of here?"

The injured man face-palmed and said, "We are talking to get out of the damn planet."

Madhav looked around hoping to see something that would give him an answer. 'I don't want to die like this.'

The injured man spoke again, "It was your idea. Now you get us out of this"

"He didn't force you to follow" Raja said.

"But he brought everyone along" the injured man screamed at Raja.

Raja took a step back.

"Maybe it's a good thing we never got a ride" the old woman said in a whisper. She had moved away from the group and was peering into an open register on the front counter. She held her mobile flash light in one hand and with the other she ran a stubby little finger down the records. "The cars do not have enough juice to make it that far."

Madhav felt a pang in his heart. He had let innocent people to their deaths.

The injured man laughed and slammed his thighs in a fit. "Those bastards. They thought we would die out here."

"How do you know that?" asked Raja.

"It says here the last cargo came in six months ago"

"Cargo" Madhav whispered, "That's it! Cargo. Sriharikota is twelve hundred nautical miles away. With a speed of 25 knots an hour…"

"…we can reach there in two days" Raja said, excitement etched all across his flushed face.

"If everything goes right" Madhav said, looking around at everyone.

"The news report said we have seventy two hours" the old woman said.

"Sixty hours." Raja added.

"We will still have twelve hours to spare" said the injured man.

"Let's go to the pier and get ourselves a vessel." Madhav said.

The four walked out of the showroom into the dark wet night.

15

4 RAINBOW IN THE DARK

Drenched in sweat and rain, Madhav led the pack forward. Through the darkness, he could make out several yachts, their long masts swaying in the turbulent waters. The sea rolled and waves crashed the pier walls, spraying them with salty mist.

Thunder rumbled in the sky, lighting the scene momentarily. Finally at pier three, Madhav stopped.

"I need your flash lights" he said aloud.

The injured man pulled out his mobile phone and turned on the flash light. The old woman followed.

"A yacht this size won't make it" The injured man said.

Madhav found his one and jumped on it. The boat bobbed up and down with his weight, "We don't need it to make it that far. Come on."

Raja took a quick look and jumped in, holding his hand for the old lady. The lady hesitated for a second.

"Madhav said, "We need a small cruise ship. And a navigator. The only way we gonna get one is over there," he stretched his hand and pointed to his right. A ball of light was visible in the distance.

"What's there?" Raja asked.

The injured man grinned and said, "The gold diggers! Brilliant!"

The yacht rocked as the injured man jumped in.

The old woman held on to the metal rails for support. "What gold diggers?"

"Those who scavenge for loot in the submerged city" Raja said in a hollow voice. He looked up at Madhav and said, "It's not such a good idea"

"Why?"

"They are mean! Uncouth and illiterate. They won't believe us."

"We'll see!" Madhav said.

"How?" The injured man and Raja said together.

Madhav smirked for he believed coincidences were lucky. That this was a sign his journey would be successful. A sign form a non-existent god. His smile faltered. It was a simple case of probability!

He checked under the cockpit and switched-on the batteries. Then he turned a key and the engine revved.

He sped the yacht out on the open waters and towards the pirate's bay. That's what they called it! The fearsome pirate's bay, inspired by the notorious Torrent website. These diggers, sixteen and seventeen year olds, were the modern day equivalents of a biker gang. Running around in their speed boats, looting any straying cargo and living a life of adventure. Looked interesting from the outside.

Madhav was too experienced to know the reality. It was a pit of vipers. He sensed Raja's anxiety. He knew these diggers were bullies. They lived in tribes named after the great band of the first gold diggers. These first diggers hit a stash of gold ornaments and jewellery in a dive somewhere between the island of Worli and the Mahim bay. Intoxicated by their success, they created a culture, much like the hippies of the west, but dangerous. They were looters. Hooligans who were not afraid to harm anyone. Soon, they captured an entire bay and made it their nest like a serpent ready to strike any ship with valuables. During the war, they became the backbone of the black markets. They had everything to offer. From razor blades to shoe laces, nothing was impossible. Madhav had made a fortune trading his Aluminium Anode batteries at exorbitant rates.

He had an ace of spades up his sleeve.

They reach the bay within the hour. It dazzled like a golden bowl as firelights glowed on every inch of the island. It was the old island of Colaba, now submerged. The area around the Gateway of India was above ground, like a tiny island.

The boys had turned the gateway into their stronghold. The 26 meter high turrets hoisted the flag of the diggers. A pixelated blue Ashoke Chakra on a Saffron background. Madhav steered the yacht on one side of the fort. The place was in sharp contrast to what the dwellers on land were used to. This was a no man's land. No rules of law applied here. The sharp yellow lights all around the fort dazzled him. A boy sat atop the stairs of the pier. He wore a leather jacket over his bare chest and a low jeans. He had sunglasses raised on his head. He was so skinny he looked malnourished to Madhav. He held up his hand to stop, brandishing a black rifle with a telescopic sight.

"Where do you think you're going?" He asked in his harsh voice.

"We need to see Raghav." Madhav said.

Raghav was the boss of the tribes of children. And a brute.

The boy stiffened and asked, "Do you have an appointment?"

"Tell him it's Madhav."

The boy flung his rifle on his shoulder and pulled out a flat, slim device. He said, "Its Madhav and friends to see your boss". Another kid with hairs like straw hurried to escort them to his boss.

Raghav was the one Madhav sold his batteries to. They had earned a fortune while the world burnt away coal to mine for lithium. His batteries needed aluminium and graphite. Raghav supplied him the raw material that he scrapped from abandoned oil rigs. Together they had earned money enough to last a decade. Raghav, in a fantastic coupe d'état, killed the two tribe heads and bought off their work force. He send half of them to work in Madhav's factory and the rest mined the rigs and worked the black markets.

They were soon escorted inside. Madhav looked up instinctively to see the ornamented ceiling of the gateway. Raghav sat high on his usual throne, a heavy wooden arm chair on top of a black teak table. A medley of stuff glimmering in the flickering light from the torch surrounded him. Raghav jumped down his seat and rushed towards Madhav, hands outstretched. Madhav gave a quick hug around his great bull neck set between massive shoulders.

"We need your help." Madhav said.

He explained him everything. He pulled out his communication device and replayed the video message of the Prime Minister.

Raghav listened with rapt attention, then he said "I'd take you, but these?"

"These are friends"

"You don't have friends" Raghav said showing his sharp yellow teeth, capped with metal.

"Look, I don't wanna leave anyone behind." Madhav said defensively.

Raghav looked at the three and pointing at the injured man said, "I don't trust this one"

"It's all of us or none. Good luck finding the evacuation point and convincing the authorities that you are a bunch of honest working citizens."

The smirk from Raghav's face vanish. He took a deep breath which looked like he was trying to compose himself.

Finally he said, "You are brave, Madhav Sharma. That's why I like you."

He turned round and picked up a flat, thin device looking like an e reader. He pressed a button and his voice echoed around the island magnified a thousand times. "All diggers from tribe Eram! Collect all the gold you have and meet us at the Pier. All diggers from Tribe David and Tribe Shantanu, prepare the Varuna. We set sail in an hour."

"Why waste time in collecting gold!" Don't you understand, nothing matters? The earth will be destroyed…" Madhav screeched.

"I'll use the gold to buy-off land on Mars. I hope you've bought your gold." And he laughed.

The Varuna looked like a cross between an old sailing ship and a cruise ship. Smaller than an ocean liner, larger than a yacht. It looked like a patchwork of rusted parts sewn together. The final look was quite menacing. The front had an ornamental Ram's head made out of bronze that glinted in the dancing flames.

"My boys made it. 1,280 horse power RAGE engines coupled with three Tesla 700 kilowatt solar power and batteries, and three water jets. Beats seventy knots an hour. Built-in GPS, auto navigation, viewer's deck and enough seats for your bottoms."

Madhav knew the chieftain liked boasting about his loot. And he was skilled with designs. "And that Ram's head?" he asked to relax his nerves.

He beamed at Madhav.

"A European traded it for his life. We intercepted his consignment for the port of Rawalpindi. Long way away from home, he was" he laughed, showing his ugly teeth again.

"You've talent. Could've made a fine engineer." The injured man said in a low voice.

"What do you mean 'could've'?" Raghav roared.

Madhav interjected with his hands outstretched and said, "You are a fine engineer Raghav. Come on be the better man."

Raghav spat. He looked at the injured man and said in a low voice that carried, "Stay away from me."

The injured man took a step back as Raghav, a mountain of muscle, towered before him, and then he walked away.

Once out of ear shot, Madhav asked him, "Why are you so hard on him? What's he done to you?"

"I don't like him." He said.

The crew of the ship were radical young kids. Most of them in their early teens, coarse and illiterate. They took orders directly from Raghav. The raucous on-board made Madhav feel like he was in a prison playground.

Madhav steered Raghav inside the cockpit, followed by Raja.

"Turn it on" he said to him.

Raghav took out a cigar, lighted it and pushed the buttons on the control. He set the location and selected the route. Then started the engines. Once out on the open waters, he released the hand wheel.

"We will go down south for Sri Lanka, turn east and cut across the Palk Strait, then turn North and head forward."

"Next stop, Sriharikota!" Beamed Raja.

✤✤✤

Madhav clutched the iron rails and looked over the skies. They were far away from the coast of Worli. The sky here was clear. He could see the thunder and clouds on the east. The starboard side is right or the left? He thought. He could hear the boys singing a song with lewd lyrics. The pool on the top deck was empty. The boys, a mix of murderers and cutthroats, used it as their lair. They tapped and danced circling the torch in the middle of the pool as if working an invisible capstan. A cool breeze touched his face. All this was about to end. The moon shone out of the clouds and the vastness of the sea took him by surprise. He wanted to capture this moment, stash it in his mind's eye forever. Then he remembered the news report. It had been three hours since the news of the failed core experiment had aired on television. They had roughly fifty seven hours left to escape. If the authorities allow them to board a spaceship that is. He didn't want to think what would happen if he was left alone, on a barren island, with the planet's core caught in a quantum explosion. But he couldn't shake it off either. He was activist before he was an opportunist. He had fought against corporations and in his glory days bought many to its knees. In his doctoral thesis he stated, "- the harm done by industrial revolution outweigh the technological advances of our race, for the race, if extinct, has no use of technology. A renewable energy revolution within five hundred years would have still repaired the planet. But corporate greed and relentless mining by nations, to prepare for a war no one needed, destroyed the very space we occupy…" Corporations across the globe condemned his views and didn't refrain to slam him as a communist. Some agencies called him a political stooge and denounced his theories. He fought on like his father. A lighting rumbled and brought him back to the present. The ship was big but not huge. He could make out Raja looking out to the sea. On the port side or starboard side? On the left of the Bow. He walked towards him, hoping to enjoy a light chit chat when he saw the injured man rise to the deck from the cabins below and disappear into the upper deck. His curiosity peaked and he went to see where he had come from. He slipped down the door inside and took the stairs to the middle deck. There were three cabins here. The first one was the Captain. The other two held the loot collected by the tribe. He went in to see the door to the treasures ajar. His eyes fell on a crumpled piece of paper. He picked it up. It was torn out of a bigger piece, one side had a round reserve bank of India seal in blue. The other side was a rough sketch of the Control Room. Madhav checked his wrist. It was twenty minutes past ten. He pocketed the note and rushed upstairs. He dashed to the control room and peered through the glass window. But there was no one inside. He ran out on the upper deck and found the injured man sing along with the gang. He looked at him and waved. Madhav waved back. He had half a mind to ask him about the piece of paper but he let it go. It had been a long day. Terrible and long. He went back to the lonely deck above the engine room and sat on the floor. The night was cool and the scent of ocean made his head feel light. He ached to talk to someone, to share his thoughts. Earlier, when he was still a young college freshman, he had a mission. He wanted the world to heal, even if had the slightest chance. He prepared a speech and named it 'Tears of Earth'. He paid the media to play it over every channel. On every video sharing platform, his speech at the convention of climate change was promoted. It was played repeatedly, so that by the time he launched his clean energy company, he had become a crusader. A rallying figure for all the activists and environmentalists. His speech had a million views around the world. He did have an ingenious idea, there was no denying that. He sold green energy, produced from solar photo-voltaic panel, pooled them and sold them via a mobile application at rates that varied like the stock market. If the demand for green energy was high, you would get a higher rate and if the demand was low, you would get a lower rate. Thus driving more and more profits towards him. He also incorporated distance and quantum of energy required to change the prices. He became so influential that his word alone could crash the stock market. Eventually, his influence became a curse. The lobbyists employed the dirtiest trick in the book to cement his fall. They termed him a conspiracy theorist. A man with no honour, someone who would do anything to get people buy energy through his application without caring if it was green energy or not. His fall from grace started with his girlfriend. She left her. And when she left, after his big fall from the heavens, he realized he didn't like her. He became indifferent to her and also to the world around him. He gave up his friends and foes and came here in Worli. He worked in the black markets and used his skills as an engineer to sell rechargeable batteries. He made a fortune. Illegal of course, but he didn't care. He was done trying to be the knight in shining armour, trying to save the world. It was better to be the mercenary, he thought. Swing the sword who ever played the best. Albeit, his fall from grace had been a very disappointing time of his life. His moral compass took a hit and all he cared about was money.

Sitting there, staring at the vast sea, he realized, inside he was the same twenty five year old entrepreneur set about to change the world. Greed, in essence, he was doomed to live with.

Madhav woke up with a start. Someone was pushing him. He couldn't move a muscle. His eyes were heavy but the person kept pushing him. "Get off me" he tried to say, but all he could do was grunt. Then, as if his frequencies tuned to normal, his eyes flew open. Raja was on top of him, "Wake up! The sun is about to rise." He gave a might shove and rolled over. The dawn was on the horizon. He didn't remember when he dozed off to sleep. They went down on the middle deck. The tribe were snoring on the floor. Madhav found the injured man amongst them. He turned to Raja and asked, "Where were you last night?"

"In the cabin under the engine room"

"And where is the old lady?"

"Locked in her cabin in the lower deck next to mine. Sea sickness" shrugged Raja.

They made their way through the swarm of bodies coiled up on the floor to the lower deck. They entered their cabins. Inside, the cabin was neat. Because it has nothing, Madhav thought. Only a mattress to sleep on. And a small oval window that opened to the sea. Madhav imagined sleeping all the way to the destination. But his heart raged like an angry bull. He took a deep breath but exhaled. It was the sea, he thought. Raja entered and sat opposite him. Madhav went back to sleep.

He didn't have to wait too long to know why he had such a sinking feeling. After the sun was up and the watches read six 'o' clock, their cabin door slammed shut. Madhav jumped and rushed to open the door. It was firmly locked. A piece of torn paper slid in. Someone had scrawled in untidy letters over a hand drawn sketch, 'stay in. You'll not be harmed.' The writer had tried to pose off as uneducated but the punctuation gave him away.

Then there was a cry from above. Then another. A gunshot fired. There was another cry for help. Another gunshot. The metal clanking of the clip hitting the floor. A terrible scream! It sounded like a lady. Then silence! Madhav and Raja looked at each other. Raja looked terrified. Madhav turned around but there was nothing he could use to defend himself. There were multiple gunshots now and screams echoed loud in the depths of the ship. Madhav couldn't bear the cries of the dead. He took a run up and slammed into the door. The door crashed and fell to the floor. He ran up the stairs followed by Raja. A thin ribbon of blood dripped from above. In the corner, crouched with his knees drawn closer, sat Raghav. He was bleeding like a waterfall. Clutching a pistol in his right hand, he gasped for breath. Madhav crawled on all fours and went up to him.

"Come on! Find him!" A familiar voice screamed from above.

"Your friend!" Raghav said between gasps, "He betrayed."

Madhav pressed his hands over his throat. Blood poured like mirth from his wound.

"I'm sorry" Madhav whispered. His clothes soaked the excess blood on the stairs. His fingers felt sticky as the blood caked.

Raghav smirked, "I don't deserve it." He said and the grin etched on his face, his eyes lost the light. He slumped and slid on his own blood to the deck below, spraying a mist of blood before dying.

Madhav gestured Raja to stay put and went up. The injured man stood in the middle of the room holding a pistol. A pile of bodies at his feet. Two boys stood as sentinel on either side of him.

"What have you done" Madhav said.

"It's all that gold and only five of us. Imagine that!"

"How could you…"

"Shut up or I'll feed you to the monsters."

"They can't be worse than you"

The injured man shoved the barrel of his gun at Madhav's face and said, "Time to die."

"How will you navigate the ship? Will they allow you to enter the city with all those blood stains and guns…?"

"You can't talk yourself out of this…"

"How did you manage this?"

"Last night, when your friend laughed at me, I knew I'd kill him. But I liked the idea of buying off a better life on Mars. Tony here, and Ulti liked my idea. Vinod died today, God rest his soul. But you see we four managed to secure all the gold for ourselves."

"By killing twenty unsuspecting kids!"

"I doesn't matter!" he roared, "I kill you and your little brother. You'll die on earth anyway. But I, I'll be a star on Mars. I'll trade my gold for a mansion and have a voluptuous girlfriend and have fun for eternity."

Madhav saw the glint of madness in his eyes.

He had seen madness before, but this! This was lunacy.

He walked out in the blazing sun with his hands above his head. The injured man shoved him on the edge. They passed an abandoned oil rig. They were near the Strait.

"You need to navigate left." Madhav said.

One of the boys laughed and said, "We know how to sail a ship."

The oil rig was close now. There was a blackened tanker on the rig's platform. It was inches away from him. Madhav turned around and said, "Let me go. You can have all the gold there is. I do not want any."

The injured man lowered his weapon by an inch. Madhav gingerly moved to his left. Raja moved behind the injured man. The two boys were looking at Madhav with their guns raised. Madhav looked at Raja and their eyes met. He gave a curt nod towards the rig, praying Raja understood. There were three of them. All armed. Raja was staring at oil rig passing by. Tears were streaming down his face. He nodded back.

Suddenly there was a brilliant flash and with an explosion. Dark, black smoke choked everyone around. Madhav slammed into the walls of the crew cabins. He smacked his head and slumped to the floor. The tank over the rig exploded, spraying flaming oil all over the sea. The ship rocked and a gun streaked across the floor. Madhav grabbed it quickly and sat up. He felt dizzy but this was no time to die. Two of the boys didn't move. The injured man took to his feet and looked around. He saw the gun in Madhav's hand and grinned. The heat from the flaming oil blazed unbearable. It stung Madhav's exposed skin like white hot needles. But he moved closer to the fire.

"I did not want to hurt you." he said.

Slowly, like a man banished by the pirates, he walked closer to the edge of the vessel. With one final look at Madhav, he opened his arms and dived into the flaming sea. Madhav looked on as the scream and the acrid smell of burning skin made him retch.

He rushed back into the shade. He longed a shower of cold water. Raja stood on the doorway to the deck going down.

"Remember you said it's not just the war, its Greed? Now I see what you   mean."

5 DAZED AND CONFUSED

Madhav locked Raja with the old lady in the cabins below and set to work. He dragged the bodies on the top deck and threw them one by one into the sea. It was horrible work. Everyone he helped ended up dead. He wiped the floors as much as he could. After a while he felt nauseated and let go. The horrible stench overpowered him and he locked himself in the cockpit. He focused on navigating the ship through the strait. The GPS blinked on. It was mid-day and the estimated time left on the screen appeared to be thirteen hours and forty minutes.

He pressed the announcement button and summoned Raja and the old lady to the Cockpit. He felt hungry. He pressed again and asked Raja if he could bring in some snacks from the pantry.

They arrived with a plate full of stale breads and packed potato chips. Madhav devoured the meal.

"We are roughly fourteen hours away from Sriharikota." He said between mouthfuls.

"What happened here is horrible," The old lady said. Her eyes were red and she looked on the verge of tears.

Madhav sighed. He took her hand into his and said, "What's happened has happened. It cannot be undone. Forget it."

She nodded. Madhav asked for more food and Raja went to get it. Eating had always been a relaxing thing for him.

Once Raja was back Madhav said, "So, what do we do next?"

"I'll sleep. Wake me up when this end." And he left the room. He had not been his usual self.

"You can wait here if you like." Madhav said to the old lady.

"I'll get some sleep too. This mode of travel doesn't suit me at all."

Before she left, she turned around and said, "Don't be too harsh on yourself. You didn't want all this to happen. It was God's will." And she disappeared downstairs.

Madhav was flabbergasted. How could she still believe in God? He pitied her innocence. She believed in the good and bad, triumph of the just and such nonsense.

The day passed uneventful and soon night crawled in. They navigated through the Gulf of Mannar and crossed the Palk Strait. The island of Sri Lanka was devoured by the sea years ago. He used it to shorten the route. He would have loved to visit the new harbour constructed at the steps of a nineteenth century Roman Catholic Church, The Shrine of St. Anthony. But they were short on time.

Sitting alone, he started to have doubts on the authenticity of the news report. What if it was all an elaborate prank? Like the 1938 radio broadcast of Orson Welles? It seemed plausible! Nobody had bothered to check. Transmission in the middle of the sea was impossible. All they could do now was wait.

At one in the morning, the GPS screen started to sound an alarm. It was time to take manual control. Madhav pressed a button and announced their end of the voyage. He managed to slow down the ship by reading the instructions on the screen. There was no harbour. They grounded on the shallow waters and laid ashore on the beach. Madhav felt foolish as he anchored. He and Raja dragged the heavy bags of Gold and the three of them walked out. There was not a soul in sight. Madhav saw a gleam of light in the distance and could make out a long, thin structure far away.

"There" he pointed.

They went through a jungle and found a long and lonesome road. They walked for twenty minutes. The road curved and there was no sign to guide them. They walked on. A while later, the old woman sat down, heaving.

"I can't walk any more" She said.

"Come on, it can't be far now. We are almost there." Raja said.

"You two carry on. I'll recover and follow the road." She said amid large gulps of air.

"Will you be all right?" Madhav asked.

The old woman nodded and held up her hand in a gesture of blessing. "You are a good man, Madhav Sharma. God bless you."

Raja went forward and touched her feet. She embraced her. Madhav, who was carrying her bag with his, put it down beside her.

"I won't need it." She said, "Take it with you."

"No. It's yours."

She sighed and said, "Carry it to the base for me. I'll take it back from you when the time comes."

Madhav picked up the bag and they set off. It was two in the morning and the night was one of the darkest. The road was in the middle of a forest alive with strange sounds. An owl hooted softly and Raja jumped. The wind howled and Madhav felt the hairs on his hand raise. The sound of a snapping twig, a starching thorn made him squint into the pitch black darkness, hiding Raja behind himself. He checked his watch again. They still had twenty six hours to survive.

Finally the road turned left and opened up to a wide patch of land. There was a tall building to the right. On the left, the road went on.

A red arrow pointed towards the left, drawn by hand and stuck up at the edge of the barren land. Below, it said The Indian Citizen Migration Program, Evacuation point. 100 meters away.

Relief. Glorious relief. The ordeal of the past two days were over. Now all he needed to do was aboard a ship and get out of here. He didn't care whatever happened to the planet.

"This is it!" Raja said, "We made it."

"Yeah," Madhav beamed.

"What will you do next?" He asked Raja.

"I'll start a restaurant." He said, "Taste-X."

"Well, I'll travel the lunar colonies. I've heard there is a check-post on the dark side of the Moon."

They had three bags each stuffed with the gold collected by the tribe of children. Madhav had calculated each bag would fetch them a Crore in international units. Good enough to start a new life.

They turned left and made their way through the clearing. The silhouette of a building with a gigantic crane was visible against the dark night sky. But the scene before their eyes made Madhav to take a step back. Hundreds of tents covered every inch of the land. People were moving about, ambling and talking. He could hear people laugh and babies cry. A couple roasted a questionable animal over a spit fire a few feet away from where he stood on the road. The smell of smoke and food mingled with a stench of strong ammonia. The area glowed with random bonfires. A booming voice in the distance announced the next flight out of the planet due in the next twenty minutes. They entered through the barbed wire security gates and walked through the labyrinth. Bottles of water, plastic cups, and crumpled paper scattered over the road. Madhav craned his neck to see any administrative tent or desk and found one. A large khaki tent in the middle. He quickened his pace and ushered Raja to move fast. Raja, after accidentally stepping in a pool of muddy water, jerked his feet and rushed to make up with him. They reached the tent. A small desk was setup at the entrance. It had a lone clipboard. A UN representative dozed off on the chair in front of him. Raja touched him and he woke up with a start.

He picked up the clipboard and the pen and without even lifting his eyes asked, "Are you listed in the IHMP?"

"The what?" Raja asked.

"Indian Human Migration Program!" He repeated with patience.

"No! We are here because of the…"

"The failed core experiment. Well done you've reached." He said snorting a little chuckle.

"Look! Can we talk to someone who can let us board a ship out of here?" said Madhav, coming straight to point. His patience with Government employees was as thin as mercy.

The man looked up to see his face. "Everyone here wants to board a ship. Register yourself and wait for your turn. Just like everyone else."

Madhav sighed, "Look! I can pay."

"You cannot pay yourself out of this one Pal." He said, "There are only eight flights and three lakh people waiting for their turn. Not counting the ones who never made it this far."

"Name?" he repeated after a few moments.

"Madhav Sharma"

"And you?"

"Raja Dixit"

He noted the names down on his clipboard and touched a button. The message beeped once and the clipboard went dark again.

"What happens now?" Madhav asked.

"Now you wait. Set up a tent or something. Go to the base over there when your name is called."

Madhav waited for him to tell him something relevant, something important. But when he didn't Madhav asked, "Where is the Intergalactic Bank counter?"

"At the base."

"How do I reach the base?"

The man exhaled, "Check the map at the end of this lane. Now let me sleep." He slammed down the clipboard and the digital pen and put his head down on the desk.

Raja led the way and Madhav followed. His hands were aching and he wanted to lie down. A sharp pain in his back tingled his nerves. He let the bags down for a moment and took a deep breath. They reached the map after a two minute walk. Madhav saw that the camp was semi-circular with the launch station at the centre. There were twelve entry gates to the camp and the road they were on led straight to the station. There was a base at the entrance and the Intergalactic Bank counter was at the far end.

He gathered his strength and picked up the bags again. He saw Raja struggle with his and offered to help lift it. Raja misunderstood the gesture and let the bag fall to the ground with a dull thud. Madhav wanted to kick him but he picked up the bag and heaved it up his shoulders. After a few minutes, Madhav felt his thighs burning with the weights. A man, poorly dressed, dirty, and with matted hair, came near them and said, "Do you need help with the luggage sir?"

Madhav ignored. He had a grating voice, like a constant sore throat.

"I can carry it for you. Just pay me a rupee."

Madhav considered him. "I don't have a rupee"

"Then give me your watch. That's a fine watch you have."

Madhav thought for a second then gave him the bags.

"The watch sir."

"Don't you trust me?" Madhav asked.

"I trust you sir but what will I do if you walk inside the base and leave me alone like the others?"

Madhav had nothing to say. He pressed the link of his watch chain and slid it down his hand. It was a gift from his girlfriend. He liked it but not enough to keep it as a memento.

The poor man took it with both hands and examined it in the flickering lights of the torches.

Then they set off again. It was a long walk. They criss-crossed through the makeshift shacks, the piles of food-cans and medical tents. The stench here was unbearable. At last they reached a big tent that had a couple of guards on duty. The poor man let the bags fall down and said, "There you go sir. The Intergalactic bank. They'll reduce your load to a piece of paper." He chuckled at his own remark. Madhav smiled weakly and moved in with Raja. Inside was exactly like the registration desk, except it was bigger. And it had a printer. A man was sitting behind the desk, sipping at what looked like coffee. Madhav looked at the steaming drink longingly.

"What can I do for you?" The man said in a pleasant tone.

"We have three bags of gold outside. We would like to receive our Intergalactic receipts."

"And what would be the amount of gold you wish to surrender?"

"About six thousand grams"

The man looked up from his clipboard. He looked Madhav from head to toe and smirked, "and where are these bags of gold?"

Madhav felt his face flush. His clothes were damp with sweat and dirty. There were dark patches all over them.

"Right here." He said and turned around. There was nothing. The bags were gone.

"All that for nothing?" Raja yelled in frustration. They searched for the bags, tracing their path back to the UN tent. They also enquired about the old man. But they both disappeared without a trace.

Nobody had seen the man they described. Madhav realized he had a thick beard, possibly to hide his features.

"If I ever find him…" Raja picked up a twig and crushed it to powder.

They walked to the common tents. The banker had advised them to go there at the center of the camp. The tent was crammed with people and none of the beds were empty. Raja disappeared and came back running to Madhav half an hour later, "There is only one bed left."

Madhav let Raja take it and went outside to sit in the open.

He roamed about the filthy streets and finally settled on a spot close to the fence. The chain-link rattled as he held it to slide down on the dusty ground. A megaphone boomed in the distance counting down to lift off. Ten nine, eight…Lift off, the deafening roar of launch vehicle and the area lit up like a wedding canopy. Madhav watched the rocket thunder and take flight. The huge spaceship mounted at the top of the rocket looked menacing even from this distance. He looked at it scarring the dark sky. He sat there for a long time gazing at it go and finally disappear.

It must have been an hour when Raja walked in with a coarse blanket and sat beside him.

"Bed bugs" he said dryly.

After a minute he said, "Who would believe. I was a millionaire for thirteen hours."

"I would" he said, patting his back.

"How does it work? Inter-planetary travel?" He asked.

"The rocket puts the spacecraft into orbit. It's called the payload. Once out of the Earth's gravitational pull, the spacecraft scans for a negative energy space…"

"What's a negative energy space?"

"Ever heard of the 'big crunch' or the 'big rip'?"

Raja looked at him with a mulish expression.

"The universe is expanding. Flying off in all directions. Consider this. If the universe keeps expanding, it will all fly away to infinity. 'Thus the big rip.' And if it is shrinking, it will collapse into itself, 'The big Crunch'. So, there must be a balance in energies for it to slow down the expansion. If there is a positive energy, there must be some negative energy space as well."

"To balance it out?"

Exactly!" He exclaimed, "You see, humans can create a negative energy space. It shrinks the space in a way that you can traverse millions of light years in a few lakh kilometers."

"Where did you learn all this?" there was awe in his voice.

Madhav smiled.

"Why?" Raja asked no one in particular. He sat there with his legs folded looking at the empty launch pad.

"What?"

"Why is this happening?"

Madhav sat there. It was quite after the lift-off. A thick smoky smell of burnt carbon hung in the air. He didn't know what to say.

A few minutes later, the megaphone sounded again. Madhav's ears stood up as he listened to the names being called. Asra Fatima, Monica D'Souza, Huzefa Mukkadam… on it went. There were millions of people waiting for their turn. He looked at his watch. They had twenty hours to survival. Less than a day. Raja propped up the blanket using sticks to look like a makeshift tent. He fit inside it, with Madhav's feet sticking out at the end.

Madhav didn't know when he dozed off to sleep. He woke up with a start when the searing heat of the sun burnt his feet. The camp was alive like a colony of ants under attack. Insistent voices pierced his ears. He turned around but Raja was gone. He checked his watch again. But his wrist was empty. He must have slept for an hour and a half.

He jumped up, fear rising to his throat like bile. What if he had missed his flight? He wanted to kick himself. He had to be at the base, trying to get in. Hustling for a flight. He left the blanket as it is and dashed towards the base. He saw swarms of people running through the filthy streets. There was a buzz of agitation and everyone was running.

Madhav caught up with a dirty looking old man and asked, "What's the matter?"

"An earthquake! Europe's been wiped out!"

Madhav stopped in his tracks, regained and started to run again. At the base people formed a formidable wall, hitting and clawing at the fence to make a way to get inside. The guard post was empty. There was no authority in sight. The crowd reached for the gate. They wanted to run away but there was no one in sight. The crowd roared to make its way, like a jungle animal. Madhav wanted to move away from the gathering but more and more people piled up behind him. He was a part of it now. They were angry, he could sense that from their movement. He rocked back and forth losing control, obeying the commands of the unseen force that brings out the worst in humans. People started to pelt stones inside the base. The glass windows of the lower floors shattered revealing an empty office beyond. The crowd pushed with all its might and the fence collapsed with an earth shattering crash.

Suddenly the megaphone crackled to life. It screeched a high pitch cry and boomed. "Everyone stay where you are! We are here for help. The Indian Space Research Organization is committed to your safety. The last Inter Planetary Flight is scheduled today at 1300 hours. The payload is restricted to twenty thousand tonnes. We have drawn out an unbiased list of people. We regret those who'll be left behind, but it's a sacrifice you must make for the race to survive. Jai Hind!"

There was a deadly silence. Then havoc wreaked! People shouted, babies cried, and the dust filled the air. They had seven hours! He launched himself forward to check his enlistment status. Where was God when everyone needed him?

He pushed himself in, shoved the men away, ducked and somehow managed to cross the sea of bodies in front of him. Sweat stuck his clothes when he reached the front lines. With a squelch, he unstuck his shirt and tiptoed to look across the wafer thin screen. It flashed a total of three hundred thousand names. He did a quick scan but couldn't see his name. He went through each name in the list. At the sixty second number, his heart skipped a beat but the name turned out to be Madan Sharma. He continued his scan. Countless names, countless numbers but none matched his. He scanned again and again but to no avail. His heart hammered against his heart as he imagined the worst possible way to die. He slumped to the ground, stunned, like so many others around him. Cries of triumph echoed with wails of despair. The world was at an end and so was Madhav Sharma, the entrepreneur, the scientist, and the activist. He had not made the list.

"Looks like you didn't make the list"

Madhav looked up. It was Raja.

Madhav nodded. He didn't want to talk to him right now. But the prospect of never seeing him again tugged at his heart and he mumbled, "Did you?"

"No." Raja said and sat beside him in the dust.

"Are we gonna die?" Raja asked.

Madhav wanted to rage at him for this stupid question. Then he felt how stupid he himself had been thinking it would be easy to board a spaceship out of earth. He had forgotten to consider other people. Millions like him trying to escape the failing planet. People who had survived the war, the famine and the epidemic. Shriharikota was the only UN designated evacuation point for South East Asia.

Now he felt ashamed. The fragility of life hit him like a bulldozer as he lay there like a spring leaf waiting for the last breeze.

"I'm sorry." Madhav whispered. Tears were streaming down his face. Hundreds of people moved in front of him, crying, embracing each other, some shrieking with joy. A low cloud of dust hung in front of him.

"You know so much about space travel. I thought you'd make it in the crew."

Something didn't add up. He looked at Raja. "What crew?" He asked.

"The crew! The interview! Didn't you see the poster?" Raja said.

Madhav's heart raced. "What poster?"

"They are looking for crew members. Anyone can apply. They are interviewing candidates right now, behind the launch pads."

"And you are telling me this now?" Madhav said as he clambered back to his feet and dusted his pants. They still had six and a half hours left to survive.

Raja sat there staring up at him with his knees close to his chest.

"What are you waiting for? Let's go!"

He jumped up and dashed.

"I thought you knew." Raja said, leading him to the interviews.

Raja moved through the crowd. Madhav had to sprint to keep up with him.

He turned and vanished. Madhav craned his neck and saw him disappear round a huge medical tent towards the base. An antiseptic smell overpowered him as he turned another corner. After about ten minutes, Raja stopped. They were somewhere behind the base. The deserted area had one entrance. It contained thick concrete walls, charred black by the soot depositing for years. Like a huge fire had burnt off everything in its wake. The sea met the sand with a rhythmic swish outside the walls.

Raja pointed a finger, "In there."

The room was empty like rest of the office tents. A table, an old chair, and a tiny ball hanging from the window to the right. A six foot three man with amber eyes and short black hair in a military regular cut sat on top of the table. He was fair and attractive. His moustache was trimmed acutely, as if with an inch tape. So precise was his appearance that Madhav felt out of place when he approached him with a handshake. A salute would have been more appropriate. He wore a white shirt with red and yellow stripes at the shoulders. A ship on a sphere was embossed on his front pocket.

'Hello!" he said cheerfully, "I'm Captain Kapil Bhama," His voice boomed inside the tiny room.

The captain took a good look at him before snatching the ball hanging on the window, "Do you know what this is?"

"I…" Madhav looked at the object in the Captain's hand. It was a small black object, no bigger than a tennis ball, with tiny markings etched all over it. He ran a finger on it and felt the metallic texture on his coarse hands. It had a tiny window covered with a half inch square piece of glass.

He returned it to the captain and said, "I do not know."

The captain cocked his head and looked at him.

"Is there something else I can help you with captain?"

The captain's smile vanished and he hinged towards him, "Son, the last flight out of here will be on a spacecraft that is a six thousand tonne behemoth. It was developed by the Inter Galactic Space Agency."

"I haven't heard of it."

"Of course you haven't. It would be a poor secret department if it were known to a common man."

"Anyways, ever since the world has decided to move out of earth, India has been looking for its own planet to migrate. We have received positive signals from a planet 40 light years away. The Integrated Space Cell has green flagged the planet but we are short of an extravehicular activity operator." He said in a hushed voice.

"Why our own planet? We have a base at Mars don't we?"

"We do. But the United Nations would not allow us to populate more than 23.6% of the space, nowhere near enough the number of people we have."

"Why?" Madhav asked perplexed.

"Well, mars is a difficult planet to survive. And considering what happened to Earth, UN is afraid we would run foul with mars too. The environmentalist made their life difficult…"

"You know what Steller Green did?" The Captain had his hands balled into fists.

"I know…" he threw up his hands in defines.

They looked at each other in silence. Then the Captain spoke, "Would you help me?"

"Considering there is time left enough for us to help each other"

"I offer you a chance to be our EVA man. That's the least you can do."

Madhav thought for a moment. He had but two choices, one was accept whatever this guy was offering and the second was being stranded on a doomed planet to die. Madhav took the Captain's hand

"I accept."

"So, what do we do next?"

The Captain regained his earlier enthusiasm.

"Let's go meet the Dragon!"

"Why do you call him the dragon?"

"During the war, he drove back 3000 Russian troop inside the enemy line. With an amputated leg!"

So the Dragon breathed fire.

He followed the Captain. He walked out of the charred room, out of the fence on the other side. They entered a twelve story building that prepared the launch vehicle. A huge yellow crane, sixty feet high, held a rocket in place with long slings strapped to the booster vessel. The building had ten iron gates, one on top of the other, that slid open to allow the crane and the rocket to move out.

The Captain crossed the launched pad and into the lift block. People talked on headsets, took notes, and talked in agitated voices. People in white coats rushed out of the way screaming instructions to the workers. A giant red clock on the top blinked away the time to launch. Madhav stopped in his tracks to admire the giant crane. A board displayed 'ISS-26, World's finest Single Stage-To-Orbit rocket.'

"Come on. We do not have time!" the captain yelled.

Madhav dashed across.

After the initial shock of the Lunch pad's colossal size, the spacecraft was a mind bender.

The Captain stopped in front of the ship and raised his hand, "That's the vessel."

The spaceship was an imposing structure. Everything looked Lilliputian in its wake.

It was shaped like three planets joined by thin bridges of glass. A long glass window ran up and down the middle giving it a union Jack kind of appearance. Thin long legs protruded from the lowest sphere.

The captain pointed at the ship and said, "Top sphere is the command centre, the two on the bottom are civilian quarters."

"This is immense" Madhav was at a loss of words. The ship was leviathan, too big to express in mere words. Its one booster was bigger than Madhav's apartment.

"How would anyone fly it?"

"I thought you knew how it works?"

"I'm an environmentalist, not an astronaut."

"Well it needs a xenon rubidium capacitor, big enough to generate negative space. It creates a wormhole between the points of travel, and sustains it long enough for it to get through." A girl said.

Madhav flipped around and saw a pretty girl with a dark mole on her chin.

"Hi Officer Shree!"

"Hello Captain. " She said.

"Then we would travel to Mars in no time." Madhav said, joining the conversation.

The pretty girl rounded on him, "It doesn't work for distances less than 5500 Astronomical Units. Too much energy lost in firing up the capacitors."

The Captain said, "We tried it once. Was stranded on an unidentified planet for eight months. Speaking of the devil…"

Clank, clank, clank.

Madhav looked around. A man in his fifties walked at him. He had a robotic leg and he walked lopsided. His face had a scar running through his forehead and half his ear was missing. The effect was menacing rather than funny.

"Admiral Ian Cordoza" said Captain Kapil smiling.

"That's the guy?" he asked roughly, pointing at Madhav.

"Yes. Admiral, I brought him here," the captain said "to be our EVA man. He fits the profile."

"He doesn't fit the profile. We do not have his psychometrics. He'd be useless on age, health, mentality, training, and temperament alone."

He turned to Madhav and said, "What skills do you have?"

Madhav looked at the two. His body ached with the long walk in the woods. His hands were still cold from the bodies he had heaved on the ship. He had but one chance to get out of this hell-hole. He gathered all his courage and said, "I'm the inventor of the quantum heat absorber."

The Admiral's face went pale and the Captain took a step back. He had spoken too soon, he thought. A nagging voice in his head said it was over.

He looked at Madhav and said, "You're in!"

6 FINAL COUNTDOWN

Attention! This is the final boarding call for all passengers. Please proceed to gate one immediately. The commander will order the spacecraft to be closed in approximately five minutes. I repeat. This is the final boarding call for all passengers. Thank you!

Madhav looked out of the window on the eighth floor. He was part of the crew now. One of the seventy five Officers selected to operate and handle the spaceship's operation. The Admiral suggested to lift the Kritikarsh to the rocket's top with the passengers. "Extra payload to lift, but easier to handle civilian crowd" he remarked when Madhav asked him the reason. Handling three lakh people was much easier on flat ground than on a sensitive and eighty foot crane. The doors were about to close. The last of the race was looking at them through the broken windows. The sea had enormous waves now, as if sensing the end was near. The sky had turned orange although Madhav knew it for a fact that it was one 'o' clock in the afternoon. An alarm rented the air. The doors were closed and the ship started to lift to the top of the booster rocket. It would take twenty minutes for the lift. Madhav stood in absolute attention. His heart palpitated against his ribs like it would break out. He had thought he was tough, that he didn't care once he was safe. But it was a lie. The girl with large eyes and a mole on her chin stood next to him in queue. She started to weep. Madhav wanted to hold her, say to her everything was all right, and that they were safe. But he couldn't. He stood there mute as a stone and gazed out. He looked out the window, down into the condemned. Madhav couldn't see out any women and children left. They all sat there, staring at the sky, perfectly still, and huddled together. He looked far into the distance. The island trembled, about to be swallowed by the sea. The birds flew erratic and smashed into the windows of the tower. Thunder rumbled somewhere in the distance, out of sight.

Suddenly there was a loud clang and the swish of sliding panels. An alarm buzzed to Madhav's right.

It was time!

The crew turned to their right, formed a single file, and marched into the canopy. The sealed translucent cover held in place by iron bends ended up into the hull of the mighty spacecraft. The imposing glass cubicle in the centre shined in the dim light entering from the mullioned windows. The giant screen at the far end reflected the elongated reflection of the crew entering through the doorway on its liquid black surface. The admiral walked in from the right, the thud of metal heavy on the ship's polished floor.

"Comrades," he screamed, "Today we fly. Not to escape death, but to find a new hope for our people. This is what we trained for! This is what we live for. This is the mission we were sent to Earth for! Remember, if we fail, we still saved enough of our race that can thrive and survive in the underground cities of Mars and whisper tales of our valour. But should we succeed, we will be the forerunners of a new civilization and the saviours of our kind. Let not this dying planet be a waste. We still have a chance to prove to the universe that humanity is capable of much more than destruction."

He looked around at everyone and cried with such force, Madhav felt the hairs on his hands rising, "Let's begin!"

The crew member dispersed into the rooms along the spherical dome and occupied their positions. Madhav marched ahead and stood behind the office marked Engineering & EVA. A bunch of people in different coloured clothes stood there already. There were two chairs left. He walked towards one and sat, fastening the seatbelt across his shoulders and into either side of the seat. The pretty girl next to him in the file entered and sat beside him without even a glance. Another alarm sounded and the countdown begun.

The ship vibrated. Madhav saw everyone holding the edge of their seats tightly. The girl next to her with a mole on her chin, looked distressed, like holding the urge to retch. The voice of the Admiral boomed into his helmet,

"Prepare for lift off."

Another voice of a woman started the countdown. Madhav found himself counting down with the rest of the crew. "5-4-3-2-1-0 booster ignition and lift-off!" The jet engines exploded below them and slammed everyone hard into their seats. Madhav had imagined it much faster, but it was not. It felt like wading through mud. After about ten minutes it gathered speed. Through the unbearable pressure and the nauseating sensation in his belly, Madhav clutched to his seat and closed his eyes.

Someone chirped on the radio, "Low Earth Orbit! Payload steady. Prepare for Trans-Martian Injection." It crackled with static.

Madhav looked on his screen. A sketch of the rocket orbiting the Earth showed.

"Second Boost Ready. Waiting for Command signal" came the muffled voice of a woman.

"Go ahead, boost us in Trans-Martian orbit." The Admiral commanded.

The helmet he wore shivered against his ears. The safety belts dug into his shoulders as if tying him to the speeding rocket. After about five hours, which seemed like a week under a heavy truck slammed over his head, the voice of the Admiral sounded again. "Activate artificial gravity. Open the safety belts. Captain Kapil, over to you."

Madhav knew they were somewhere in space but traveling to Mars was not like traveling on Earth. He knew that the spacecraft must be at a precise angle to the planet to make the entry and safe landing. And Mars must be aligned with the position of the Earth. He had a vague feeling that space travel was not dependent on the planets aligning any more. The team behind him was active. The tiered seats with screens embedded on their tables were either busy in calculations or pulling levers on their console. Finally a voice in the radio said, "Heliocentric longitude aligned."

"Turn on the boosters and course correct!" shouted the girl next to Madhav. Her voice sounded shrill on the radio.

After a tiring one hour of course correction and alignment, the journey to the red planet began. A voice on the radio said,

"Ladies and gentlemen, this is the Kritikarsh Indian Human Migration Flight 801. My name is Captain Kapil and I'm your chief flight attendant. On behalf of the commander of the ship Admiral Ian Cordoza and the entire crew, welcome aboard. We have completed the trans-orbit at a hundred nautical miles above Earth.

Our flight time will be of 255 hours and 45 minutes. We will be flying for Mars which will be 67 million miles away.

At this time, make sure that your seat belt is correctly fastened. Artificial gravity for civilians will be turned on in approximately five minutes. Your journey to Mars has begun. Thank You"

For the next four days, Madhav hardly moved. He sat there on his cushioned chair observing the pretty girl with long hairs and a mole. She

never smiled! He looked on as she pulled the lever and course corrected the spaceship every morning, making complex calculations on the screen. He asked her what these were.

"Spaceship trajectory. This is a dynamic spaceship for long distance travel. We can change the trajectory and destination anytime we want."

"So why do you change it so often?"

"The weight of this ship if huge. It strays off the target."

"What happens if we stray too far?" Madhav gulped, sensing the answer even before she replied.

"It will wander off-target and we would wonder how to enter Mars's orbit without collateral damage."

Breakfast was bleak on the ship. They had to take the mandatory green and rubbery capsules labelled Spirulina.

Although the food was mediocre, dinner was the most exciting part of the day. The engineering crew sat together, talking and discussing! The Lieutenant Commander was a lively man with fascinating war stories. The other departments joined in and everyone had a lively time. Captain Kapil was a regular. So was Petty Officer Rina from medical, a tall and petite general physician who had a thing for white haired men. Once she noticed Madhav, she sat beside him and told him about stuff that didn't matter even to the crewman on janitorial duty. Madhav smiled and endured. He didn't want to be left out.

Twice, he went out to the civilian quarters to look for Raja. But the ship was too big a place to find a teenage boy and an old lady, if the lady had made it at all.

The civilian quarters were in total contrast to the command area. The aisles littered with food packets and old stuff, mostly discarded clothes. Eight decks rose in spiral inside the sphere, connected with four elevators on either side. The fourth deck had a viewing gallery that provided an appalling view of dark dead space.

On the third day, when Madhav was ambling in the viewer's deck, he met Captain Kapil in a track-suit, drenched in sweat.

"Hello Captain. We will be reaching Mars tomorrow isn't it?"

"Yes" he said with a wide grin, "Tomorrow starts your training."

Madhav looked around at him, "Answer me this captain, there must have been a million earthlings on Mars. What made you search for recruits from a pile of humans on a doomed planet? I'm sure you would have found a better men on Mars."

The Captain turned to look at him, "Aren't you happy to be alive?"

"I don't understand why would you look for recruits at such a moment."

The captain turned to look outside. Far away, red dot light sparkled like a gem. The civilians aboard the ship stirred. A group of old men passed the two, jogging in their dirty clothes, looking at the little red dot in the distance.

"I'm not the right person to answer this question."

The Captain's face was set in stone. Madhav sensed something was wrong and asked again, "How many men did you recruit?"

The Captain flashed his eyes and said, "Keep patience, you'll know the truth, Madhav Sharma."

Madhav had not expected an answer. He knew from the look on the Captain's face that he was rather pushing his luck. He dropped it and thought of the underground colonies of Mars.

On the third day, Madhav set forth for the viewer's deck as usual for his routine jog. He was not an early riser, but the events of the cruise ship didn't allow him a sound sleep. He gave up after a few hours of tossing and went back to the viewer's gallery. The deck was empty. The red dot was larger now, as big as a full moon. He could make out an enormous mountain jutting out of the surface. Its peak reached out of the planet and into the space. It shone with the light off the sun and looked like an odd alien base. Like a control tower. Far to its right he saw deep gouge marks. It looked like a giant furrow flowing through the land. It looked like a big ball of copper suspended in the vastness of dark space.

They entered low Martian orbit by the end of the day. The crew was back in action. Shree, the pretty girl next to him sent a signal to the Martian base for authorization.

They designated the Nier crater for landing with a countdown of ten hours.

Ten hours later, Shree confirmed the altitude at three hundred kilometres and a near circular two hour orbit. The Admiral green-lighted the descent. They entered the braking altitude, and slowed down.

Although everyone was strapped to their seats, the last minute of descent was horrible. The sound of the ship tearing through the artificial Martian atmosphere was deafening.

And   with   a   loud   thud,   they   landed.

7 KEEP YOURSELF ALIVE

They landed at the crater. A huge conduit that looked like wet plastic connected to the twelve exits of the craft. The white canopy dazzled in the bright sun. Madhav followed the engineering crew out of the spaceship. There were transparent windows inside the conduit through which people were staring out. It smelled like mothballs and wool. Kind of like antiseptic. He saw huge twenty feet walls all around and figured they had actually landed inside a big dust bowl below the surface. They walked for fifteen minutes when the conduit started to slope downward. The landscape disappeared. It was dark in here, illuminated by cool white lights on top of the canopy. The path here was grated with slim steps that seemed to discourage running down the lane. Madhav walked behind one of the engineers from his team and could easily look over his shoulder. At last he could see lights at the end of the tunnel. He could hear the buzz of chatter, the pushing of trolleys and babies crying. It was no different. He felt home. The colossal weight on his heart that stabbed him ever since they had left earth seem to loosen. Home is where there is family. The tunnel opened into a huge walled chamber with a high ceiling. People were swarming out of every corner into the middle of the hall. There was a security desk behind chrome barricades. A flock of guards in uniform, checking every individual with a probe. Behind the barricades, Madhav could see a cabin with huge approachable windows. A golden lettered banner on top said "Migration Registration Counter - Martian Federation." Some had already made it to the desk, their luggage held into one hand carelessly. Children ran around the lofty halls beyond while the parents haggled with an old woman behind the screen. A guard at the end of their tunnel shuffled the crew members into a different queue. Madhav craned his neck in hopes to catch a glimpse of Raja and the woman they had left behind. But there were too many people. He hoped once he'd reach some place to stay, he'd search for him. Soon, he was the next in line. The guard checked him with the probe that looked like a tennis racket. It printed out a slip of paper from a slit in its handle. He tore it into two, impaled one on a rusty little nail on the gate and gave him a copy. He looked at it and moved forward absent minded. The slip had his medical data. It mentioned his blood group, allergies and a note. The note had some cryptic looking words that seemed more appropriate on an ancient roman tombstone. He looked around and saw that there was no registration desk for the crew. Most of them hurried past him, turned a corner and disappeared. Madhav caught sight of Captain Kapil and lurched after him.

"Hello buddy!" he said in his usual cheerful manner, slapping a large hand on Madhav's back.

"Where do we go now?" he asked.

"Oh! Er, you go to the training compound with the rest of the new recruits."

"Are you going there too?" Madhav asked with hopes of tagging along.

"No. I go to the officer's mess. But I'll see you around. I'm one of the trainers"

"Really! What do you teach?"

Captain Kapil rolled his eyes and looked at him with a 'haven't you guessed already' smile.

"NEW RECRUITS OVER HERE", a sharp yell from behind Madhav sounded.

"That's your cue" the captain said and disappeared with the rest.

Madhav turned around and saw a thin hawk like girl in kahkis. A troop of fifteen crewmen surrounded her. Madhav dashed along with another man and joined the ranks.

She stood in the centre of the ring with hands behind her back. She said in a crisp voice, "I'm Laika, your supervisor for the next ten days. Thirteen of you will make the crew and four would be backup. You will be accessed for the positions of Crewmen Apprentice. You'll work for Department of Supply, Spacecraft maintenance, Combat system or Engineering."

One amongst them shouted, "Who decides what we do?"

"The training does. There will be an assessment before you start. We have only 240 sols that is about ten and a half earth days."

A round of excited murmur went round the group. The man next to Madhav said in a low voice, "Why are they in such a hurry?"

The voice carried because Laika turned towards him. She said in a sharp voice that carried clearly over the buzz of chatter, "You'll know everything when its time. So, everyone got their med slips?"

"Yes" everyone chanted.

"Good. Now go get those shots from the dispensary." She pointed to where the Captain had disappeared, "and board the underground to Indus Vallis." She handed them a leaflet. The paper flapped unnaturally in the Martian gravity. The spaceship had already lowered the artificial gravity on the ship to match the base conditions twenty fours ago. Madhav didn't have any problems in confronting Martian gravity. The leaflet was an instructional sheet on how to reach the ISRO training academy. He went with the rest of the trainees and got a jab on his forearms. Something like liquid fire streamed through his body. The doctor was an aged man with grey hair and a face full of white beard. The dispensary was small, white with a cabinet full of labeled glass bottles. The doctor took out a small vial with a swirling white liquid and forced a needle over the rubber cap.

"You'll feel a burning sensation for a twenty four sols." He said stabbing Madhav's left arm.

"Sols?" Madhav asked lowering his sleeve and dabbing the puncture with a cool cotton swab.

"Martian time. I reckon you adjust your watch. It's important that you rest for this to work. If you feel nausea, hallucinations or fever, report to the nearest medic immediately."

Outside, the recruits, all in varying state of shabbiness, talked excitedly. He felt like he was back in school. He boarded the underground train with the gang and reached the city of Indus Vallis in one and a half hours. The train never hovered on to the surface. It seemed everything was under the ground. Outside, the station walls looked like black granite. The complex throbbed with youngsters, reading, smoking, and walking around. It was like a bee hive. The humans were also different looking. Lean, pale and red eyed. The girls were skinnier and taller than their Earthly peers. They wore colourful clothes and most of them had thick jackets over their shirt. The recruits climbed a flight of steps and the station opened up to a wider complex. It had shops on all corners and people swarmed in and out of the place. A man was selling samosas in the corner. The whiff of fresh cooked potatoes lingered in the air. Madhav felt his mouth water but he didn't have any money. He wondered what they would get to eat, or would they be fed at all!

He opened the instruction leaflet. In the dim light he saw that they were right under the academy. He looked around and found a pair of elevators on his right. The other recruits also discovered the elevators and lined up in front. They went in. The elevator dropped instead of rising and the atrium disappeared from sight. At the minus fourth level, the doors slid open and they entered a narrow hallway with a dirty white carpet. At one end, two guards with the racket probes were sitting on a desk that looked like black plastic. The guard frisked everyone and collected their med slips punched by the dispensary. The entrance hid behind the desk in an alcove. A heavy metal door with a circular glass window.

Inside, a narrow carpeted hallway with office like cubicles on either side ran down the length of the hall. The ceiling was low and for a second Madhav ducked trying to save his head. He saw a small cabin to their left beside a bunch of work desks labelled ADMIN. An idol of the Elephant God, Lord Ganesh with fresh incense peeked out of the transparent walls of the cabin. On the right a door marked CONFERENCE HALL. It was quite inside. So silent, Madhav could hear the hum of air conditioner running in the background.

Further down the narrow corridor the room split into two symmetrical spaces. The roof here seemed lower. Stacks of cardboard boxes and paper bundles piled up from the racks embedded on the walls. Laika reappeared from one of the side cabins. She split them in two groups and led one to the left side cabins, reappeared and took the other to the right side. Madhav choose a seat close to the aisle. The last person here had put up a sticker of Lord Jagannath on the front panel. The gang settled on the soft cushioned office chairs.

"The last page of your leaflet has an encoded chip. Touch it on the scanner and enter" she pointed to the glass cabin at the ADMIN block.

She called out names and people left for their interview. The gang was a mottled group of scientists, mechanics and repairmen. Everyone had army training, which was not uncommon. Most Indians served the armed forces for a minimum of three years. Madhav had his patriotism questioned in college when he didn't sign up. But it was a matter of choice and he thought he knew better ways to serve the nation. But his father threatened to sever all ties with him. He joined, but his superiors always found odd jobs for him to perform. Jobs that didn't need much work. He had with great difficulty, finished his course and joined civilian life.

Madhav thought about all the stuff he had done in his life. He rehearsed an interview with someone like the Admiral but faceless, asking questions he could answer. Then he realized this was a space exploration program. He would have to answer stuff that would make him useful for the campaign. He started to muse things a space exploration team might need from an engineer. He'd tell them about his battery. And his skills with the solar panels. That would be useful.

Within one hour, it was his turn to enter. He got up from his seat, scanned the leaflet, and pushed open the door.

Inside was white. The Ganesh Idol was not visible anywhere. In fact, the room didn't look like what it appeared from the outside. There was a leather arm chair and an ornate wooden table at the far end of the room. A pale man sat with his legs crossed, dressed in a black suit. His hairs were like straw, and his hands were like that of a spider, thin and long. He was skinny and hard to look at.

"Madhav Sharma" he said in a thin low voice and gestured him to sit across. He took out a thin black tablet and scrolled with his long fingers. He gave a grunt of satisfaction and tapped on the screen.

"You have a stellar record. Three years in the Mahar regimen, PhD in environmental science, masters in electrical drives."

He kept flicking through the screen, "And the CEO of oh..." his face fell. He looked up at him and tilted his head, "You could have bought out a dome here? Why didn't you?"

"I wanted to stay behind and observe the effects on Earth."

"And what did you observe?"

"Well, the heat became unbearable, more humid. The weather became harsh. The mosquitoes got pretty big, and the water striders, almost giant."

The man laughed. A cold laugh. Madhav hesitated and as soon as he chimed in, the man stopped laughing.

He picked up a blank sheet of paper and waved it in front of Madhav. "Do you know why they call it a foolscap paper?"

He tapped the screen once more and the printer jazzed on the table. It shot out a sheet of paper. The man snatched it and twirled it in his hands.

Madhav nodded side to side, "No sir, I don't"

"In fifteenth century Germany, the printer would make a Jester's Hat as an identification for its standard size and quality. You know, for brand recognition and to stop counterfeit. The Jester's hat or Fool's Cap became the symbol for this size and thickness. His competitors started to call him a fool and the paper a fool's cap. For they thought standard product will never catch-up. I don't blame them, the printing press in those days, used reels of papers. But today, you can print anything, anywhere. They slandered his name but it became the standard. Etched in stone."

He gazed at Madhav.

"The name doesn't represent you, your work does! Nobody gets a second chance. But here you are."

"I don't get it..."

"Oh! But you do. Don't you? You regret what your invention did to our planet. You tried to stop it, being the chauvinist hero you like to play, but it wasn't enough! Was it?"

"But it was out of my control! What could I have done?"

"You know how fake those words are. You could have stopped it if you didn't lack conviction. Somewhere deep down inside, you wanted to know what would happen if they accessed the core."

He felt the anger rising to his face as it became hot.

"Wrong! I knew the experiment would fail. Quantum manipulation is highly probabilistic under such high pressures. I wanted them to fail, for what they did to me. I was the founder of the enterprise. It took me ten years to discover the quantum manipulation effect. I invented the first quantum shield. The one that you use to power these colossal ships that saved all our asses."

He had worked himself to a fury and his heart palpitated. The man sat motionless, looking at Madhav through knitted brows.

"But I could have stopped it! I warned them over and over again. Greed blinded them. " Madhav sighed.

"Here is your chance to redeem yourself. I assign you Planetary Strategist and Extravehicular Activity Engineer. But for the next ten days, you'll have to clear all the fifteen subjects and prove yourself as worthy." He handed him the paper.

Madhav took it and said, "I'll do justice."

"I hope you don't fail this time." He gestured him to move out.

Laika snatched the paper from Madhav and held it up in front of her eyes, "What did you do in there?"

"Why?"

"He has set all the subjects for you. That's seventy five credits. Five for each of the fifteen subjects."

"I don't see a problem here?"

"You need to earn sixty credits or above! He must hate you."

She shoved the paper back in his hand. The gang gathered back after the interviews and led deeper into the hall, back to their workstations.

After a brief welcome message from the director of the institute, Laika took them to their quarters. They walked through the long hall, into a thin passage. A metal door with a round glass window separated the training quarters from the main hall. The walls of narrow passage curved left to the rooms above. The walls held fire extinguishers and Janitorial supplies. A huge vacuum cleaner that sucked off the Martian dust every hour, hummed in the corner taking up most of the space.

On the right was the canteen.

"One hazelnut coffee and a Mumbai Vada Pav. Can I get anything else for you sir?" The waiter said slamming the tray like a dull routine. He wore a white headdress, the end of the turban dangled to his waist.

"No, Thank You. Where does so much electricity come from? And where did you get all these food!"

The waiter smiled. "There are huge farms on the surface. You must visit them while you are here." And he hurried back to attend the queue. One of the recruits joined Madhav. He had a tray full of red pasta and a mug of tea.

The whiff of tomatoes caught Madhav.

"I have been asking around. This is the landing site of NASA's Cassini spacecraft. Right above the Cassini crater. The federation of Mars has built huge hydroponic farms and solar power plants on the surface."

"That's interesting."

"Yeah! Why would anyone want to leave this planet? Anyways, we are planning a trip to the surface tonight. Would you care to join?"

"I'd love to but I have work to do."

"Come-on man. Training sessions hasn't even started yet!"

He caved-in. The man, Ratan, opened a tourist map on his communication device that had the IHSP logo on it.

"Where did you get that from?"

"Didn't you register? You have to submit your letter and collect the kit. I hope the lady hasn't left already. She was grumpy as a frog, croaking about the hours of darkness she has to endure. It's horrible the way she said it."

"I'll go" and with that he dashed back to the workstations, clutching the foolscap paper in his hand.

Sure enough, a lady sat there murmuring to herself. Madhav didn't blame her. She was so frail and tiny it was hard to notice she was there. He handed in his paper and the lady looked at him daggers.

"You are late! And you wish to be an explorer. Shame on you."

"I'm sorry."

"On a mission in space and you managed ignored a full grown human. Good luck to you sir."

She slammed the paper on a square box and pushed a button. It glowed and gobbled up the paper. Then, Madhav heard a whirring of cogs somewhere below his feet and a black suitcase appeared on the desk.

"That's yours." She said pointing to the case in a sort of dull routine.

A door flew open and a dozen of the staff appeared from the conference room. One of them rushed to the counter and turned on a screen attached to the pillar. It showed a bright speck of light on a dark background.

"What's that?" his curiosity piqued.

"They say it's the Earth. It's gone."

Every screen in the office replayed the image. The reporters touted it as the darkest moment in human history. Indeed, blowing up a planet required expertise. Soon the deep space observer telescopes on Mars came up with detailed pictures of a Planet. Earth looked like a ball of fire. Hot lava trickled down every inch of the cities and towns, twisting everything to a molten sludge. Madhav imagined people melting, the skies dark with smoke, ash raining down.

That night Madhav and the gang went to see the city of Cassini. An elaborate labyrinth of brick alleyways criss-crossed all around the underground station. Yellow lights, encased in glass balls, illuminated the pathways. The arches and the brickwork reminded him of European towns, gobbled up by sea centuries ago. Now alive only in encyclopedias. At first, Madhav thought the walls were painted red and blue in a similar pattern. He took a closer look. They were all posters of the same man in red and blue colours. A man with a short beard holding a flag that said 'Free The Colonies'.

The gang visited the shrine to Elon, the God of space travel. He rode a car into space, hands wide open, one leg over the dashboard. A halo over his space helmet. An array of flowers, and cards lay there. Scented candles and incense sticks filled the shrine with sweet aroma. Golden pipes fended off the front of the pavilion. People were weeping on the streets, offering flowers to the shrine. A woman close to Madhav cried in loud sobs. The agony of losing their home. It was a sad night. A drone attached with a loudspeaker announced a gathering in solidarity of losing their home planet. A little while later, thousands of people came out on the streets. They moved towards the huge Atrium at the station. This was not a mob. Not like the rioting gang of the refugees, nor the aggressive band of city dwellers. This was a congregation. There, this crowd of humans held hands and offered their silence to mother Earth.

Next day, they went through a physical examination routine. A fleet of men in uniform scrutinized every document, certificate, and ID. One lady wore an eyepiece and examined their fingerprints and matched it with the biometric. They prodded and poked the recruits for two and a half sols. Laika appeared and gave a speech, more like a monologue, to discourage any faint hearted before the final bell. "Congratulations! You are the last recruits from Earth. You will join the exploration mission two hundred and sixteen hours from now as Crewman Apprentice. I'll not lecture you what to do or what not to do in this crash course, but I'll say this - this is not a vacation or a romantic getaway! You might think that all it takes to be an explorer is a sharp mind and agility. The first Martian crew needed that. But a crewman today is a specialist. A highly skilled one-man-army. He basks in the imperfection of things. The crappier the problem, the happier he is. This work is dangerous makes them value their life because of the price they paid for it!

Be prepared for loneliness, because as far as I know, we are alone!"

The training sessions were series of advanced lectures on astrophysics. Madhav had to endure ten more on semantics, engineering, astro-biology and so on. The sessions were tiring but Madhav enjoyed working out the problems.

Ten sols and a whole lot of lectures later the training was over.

Madhav and the gang graduated as apprentice. They signed a stack of paper with declarations and it took almost six hours before they set foot out of the academy. The gang visited the hydroponic farms inside steel containers. Anti-gravity cesium solar panels that also worked in night made up the roof of these containers.

The final meeting with the Admiral happened the next day. At the last minute before re-entering the spacecraft with all the crewmembers present.

The Admiral's speech lasted a full thirty seconds.

He was not a man of much words that was clear. Madhav could swear he saw the Admiral wink at him. They once again entered the Kritikarsh. It looked much smaller now with only the hull and the control ship. Once again the doors closed behind them. They took their places and fastened the seat-belts. Shree sat beside Madhav, clad in her usual white with green stripes.

The Admiral said in a booming voice, "Start Lift-off"

They waded through Mars's wafer thin atmosphere and reached the orbit in two hours. Madhav was surprised to see the rocket in action. Earth was much more difficult to escape. The Admiral's voice echoed once again and he said, "Fire us to T-786, Shree"

The pretty girl next to her jumped into action. "Xenon Rubidium capacitors online"

A man to his right said, "System status OK! Dielectric OK! Capacitor set. Ready to fire on command!"

Another man said, "Path identified. 46 jumps iterated. First jump Quadrant A 2-o-2 x, 216 y, 543 z to Quadrant N 2-0-2 x, 616 y, 595 Z"

Voice of the admiral boomed, "Fire up the caps!"

The girl pushed some buttons and traced her finger on the screen on her table. "Caps powered up for Quadrant N 2-0-2 x, 616 Y, 595 Z! Ready for discharge."

"Lithium Chronitron Limiter in circuit"

"Searching for negative space"

There was a loud buzz like a lightning strike. Madhav looked around. Shree stared at her screen, making complicated hand movements. Others behind him were busy pressing the buttons and sliding bars on their touch screens.

A man at the top of the stepped room said, "Negative space generated. Preparing the wormhole!"

He pulled a lever and Madhav felt his head shrink to half its size. His chest heaved and burnt. His throat choked and for a second his vision blurred. Then as suddenly as it happened, he could breathe again. He gasped and took in a mouthful of artificial oxygen.

"Wormhole stable, Boosters ready! Launch in 5-4-3-2-1"

The ship escalated. Madhav, though bound to his chair with two crossed safety belts, felt the tremendous speed of the spacecraft. The view around him seemed to melt away, his body pushed back deep into the cushion of his seat. And he couldn't move a muscle. The ship continued through the wormhole for five hours. Finally, Shree pressed a button and said, "Quadrant N reached. Ten seconds to destination."

Madhav counted down with her and the ship slowed down. When it was safe to open the seat-belts again, Madhav felt his limbs go numb. He wanted to and feel the blood flow back into his brain.

The Captain shrieked, "Officers! Be ready! Do not let Nestergia to set in"

He turned towards Shree and asked, "What's that?"

"Untrained recruit?"

Madhav felt blood rising to his cheeks, "No!"

She rolled her eyes, "Nestergia is the negative energy from the caps that sets in your muscles and paralyzes you"

"Paralyzes?"

"Yes. And eats away your ligaments."

"That doesn't sound good."

She didn't answer and kept fidgeting with the screen in front of her like playing an intense video game. Madhav hoped she would say something. His curiosity piqued.

The ship was stable now and he saw the engineers taking off their helmets and chatting with each other.

The Voice of the commander boomed again on the radio, "Ship stable. All activities to normal."

The girl took of her helmet and jerked her thin long hairs out of her eyes. She undid the safety belt, stood up and looked around.

Madhav gave her a smile and said, "Hi, I'm Madhav! Madhav Sharma."

"I'm Shree." She said with a stone face and turned away. He felt stupid.

8 ACROSS THE UNIVERSE

On the ninth day, after the five hour haul through the worm hole, the Lieutenant Commander sent for an emergency meet. The spaceship stranded in mid-flight, needed repairs. Shree reported problems with course correction. The ship wasn't moving. A dull silence filled the craft, which otherwise buzzed with the whirring of the machines.

Whatever he had imagined, he didn't think he'd need to be out there so early in the journey. He had always thought extravehicular activity commenced after landing or as scouts. Shree took charge to investigate. She formed a team of two apprentice, one from maintenance and one from engineering. Ratan andMadhav volunteered! The team led by Shree went down to the hull. As Madhav traversed the floors below, the control panels loomed to his right. The silence of the generators felt like a sleeping beast. Madhav adored being in here. He stood there, gazing at the futuristic monsters that pumped the radioactive element to generate the wormhole. Through these wormholes the ship traversed infinite space in mere seconds. The glass-walled testing terminal room stood high atop a tower in the centre of the hull. As he and Ratan climbed the grated steps, he looked upward at the glass workstation. It was a small hundred square-feet room, carpeted and air conditioned, with a giant screen split in two. One side of the screen had a console open with lines of code blinking every second. The other side displayed a three dimensional figure which, Madhav recognized from his training, as the Plutonium-238 housing chamber.

Ratan typed in a command and the image on the right zoomed in on a section of the device, "The power supply is OK! The Xenon-Rubidium

Capacitor is OK! The Quantum Drive is OK! The Lithium Chronitron limiter is offline."

He zapped some lines into the console. It beeped and went blank for a second. Then a screen full of information appeared. On the right, the image zoomed in further and stopped at a U-shaped silver pipe.

"The triolic quantum drive is offline. We need to re-pipe the plasma to the xenon rubidium capacitor cleaner."

Madhav looked at Shree with wide eyes, "Re-pipe the plasma! We will have to get on top of the main deck!"

"That's right. Get out there and get it back online!" Shree added.

"But that means I'll have to spacewalk."

"Is there a problem officer?"

"No' Madhav said.

Shree, with Ratan, prepared a detailed report of the error. Shree prepared an itinerary of tools and equipment. She filed the papers in one bunch and said, "Hand this over to the supply department. Take this other form to Captain Kapil and enrol for a fortnight's training."

"Training?" Madhav asked. In a spacecraft full of explorers and scientists, was there none who could spacewalk?

His query was answered soon. The Captain was enthusiastic when he received his request.

"Ah. So you are the man chosen for the repair!"

"Why, Captain, is there no one on the spacecraft who can fix this? Why do we have to wait for twenty Earth days?"

"Er, this unit was haphazardly put together to set up a base on an alien planet. We are more like space combatants."

"We do not have scientists on the crew?"

"We have, but this is his first flight."

"Why would ISRO send such a crew on a mission?"

"Look we had to get rid of a few recruits. They were not many people willing to go forth with this mission." He said as if each word caused him pain. There was something the Captain was struggling to keep a secret. And the Crew was happy serving the Admiral.

In a bitter tone Madhav said "This mission is working only on loyalty to the Admiral. But we both know loyalty alone doesn't pay." He wanted to train and go forward with the skill. But the incompleteness of the crew made him uncomfortable. Like a splinter in the tooth out of your tongue's reach.

"Start your training. You'll know ever thing there is when the time comes." The captain said with a tone that meant the conversation was over.

Madhav's head was burning with questions. He felt cheated to be sent on a space exploration mission with Army men and a naive scientist. But he had respect for the captain and so he continued.

That's when his true training began. For two weeks, they were stranded in the endless void of space. And for two weeks, Madhav was under water. The Kritikarsh Training wing had a massive 40 feet deep pool, a hundred feet wide and as long as the main hall, one hundred and fifty feet. Inside was a miniature xenon-rubidium capacitor engine. Wires and cables jutted out of it like a water creature. Madhav spent ten hours on it every day for fortnight. For the first three days, everything was normal. He'd spent time in the pool and rewire the miniature hull. He'd strip it down and visualize the drive while Captain Kapil kept a silent vigil, measuring his vitals. Before the weekend, people flocked to see him work. They would whisper and stop talking awkwardly whenever he came near them. People would stare him down and whisper behind his back. By the end of the second week, people started to question his recruitment. Captain Kapil took the onus and pushed him to his limits. He'd be in there fifteen hours a day and the Captain would make him toil endless laps around the pool in his weird baggy suit. Madhav could sense the tension of the crewmen. Stranded for two weeks, limited provisions and a false promise made this as good as a pirate ship up for mutiny. Madhav out in more research into his labour.

Finally, he managed to get the entire itinerary prepared by Shree perfect in one go. The next day, the Lieutenant of his division approved for the spacewalk. He hardly slept that day. The alarm went off while he had dozed off to a soft sleep. He woke up and jogged on the fourth floor viewer's gallery. A constellation of five stars that looked like a crown on a head shined through the starboard side of the gallery. He'd be up-close to it in a few hours. He barely ate any breakfast which was good in a way as the taste of all this packed food was nowhere near Bhati's kitchen. The Lieutenant insisted him to take a couple of white pills labelled Spirulina. He held one and the capsule crumbled spilling blue coloured powder all over his shirt. It was common for the vitamin and protein pills to disintegrate. He fished out another one from the blister pack and swallowed both in one go.

The captain waited for him in the changing room. With his infectious smile he said, "Gravity inside the ship makes you feel dizzy when you float upside down in the pool. Out there, there's no up or down. Try to enjoy it while you can!" he said before giving him the orange jumpsuit.

Madhav's hands trembled. He pulled up the orange jumpsuit over his right leg while juggling on the left. It was like a jute bag. He felt the criss-crossed threads of material over his gloved hands. He took the helmet that tethered to a spike on the inside wall, and pushed-in his head. He walked towards the exit chamber. The small room closed and he was locked inside. The computer activated a vacuum pump that sucked out the air and filled it with Nitrogen. The computer, on cue from Petty Officer Shree, opened the space gate. Madhav felt his muscles go numb. He could sense the commands his brain received to move his arms, he flexed his fingers in front of his face. He saw them contract and expand but he couldn't feel them.

The next four hours, he floated in space. With an array of tools he connected the plasma carrying tubes to the drive head. He sent a curt message to check the status. The ship refused to budge. It floated free in space, with nothing to stop it.

His helmet buzzed and Shree screamed, "If we don't correct the course, we wouldn't have enough fuel to get back to the base."

Madhav went to each booster and checked. The lithium in the Quantum effect Limiter absorbed the excess energy of the drive. It heated up to maddening heights. The fluorine plasma circulated as a coolant and disposed-off the extreme heat. For the engine to start, it was essential for every equipment to work in perfect synchronization. Even a slight calibration mistake had the potential to stall the propulsion. He floated weightless in space and looked around. Metal spikes jutted out of the sides to provide access to the top of the engine. He grabbed a spike and pulled his body forward. The tether cable tangled around his left leg. He pulled it free and held the next spike in line. Slowly, he kept reaching for the spikes and pulled his mass closer to the engine head. He checked the calibration head of the limiter.

And then it hit him!

He started towards the limiter circuit at the top of the ship.

Ratan's voice echoed across his helmet, "Where are you going!"

"Ratan, let me check the limiter…" Madhav tried to explain.

Shree barged in, "Officer, just do what's in the itinerary!"

"I know what I'm doing…"

"You are an apprentice! Do not attempt anything that can put the mission in danger!"

"Believe me officer, I know what I'm doing." Madhav said, "You have a Fluorine based Plasma to cool the cleaner drive."

"So?" Shree said in a shrill voice.

"So, Fluorine reacts with Lithium. Don't you get it?"

He cut off the radio. He could hear the screams of a reluctant Shree but he ignored. He needed a cool eye to spot the problem and rectify it. He'd have to float to the top of the spaceship, reach the tallest tower housing the limiter, and descent back inside the alcove of the capacitor. It was strange floating away in space. He grabbed a pipe and swinging on it, dove towards the alcove. He prayed the tether was strong enough to hold him back. He reached the top corner and for the next half hour, calibrated the circuit. Satisfied, he flicked the radio on and asked for the status.

There was a pause and then loud noise erupted on the radio. Ratan screamed, "It's on-line!"

After the spacewalk, he shot to fame. That evening, Reena Yadav, a medical officer, which had two crew members, asked him out for a fun evening in her camp. She kept ogling at him, nodding on his comments and laughing hard on trivial matters. Madhav soon excused himself and joined Captain Kapil on his discussion with Shree.

"So, when the isotopic ray is offline, we should eject the gamma lubricator and increase the variance of the ionic power brackets."

"What's an isotopic ray?" Madhav asked, trying to blend in before Reena saw him.

Shree turned to look at him. She stood there with pursed lips and folded hands. Madhav returned a weak smile.

"It's a kind of a gun. It blasts an energy surge like a bullet. Effective against walls, rocks, mountains - pretty much everything, except organic life." The Captain said.

The Captain turned back towards Shree, "If we increase the intensity of the charge? It might make it lethal."

"That just might." Madhav said.

"You see! Madhav thinks it's the right idea." Captain Kapil beamed.

Shree knitted her brows and asked rather rudely, "and how would it work?"

"Well, with enough ionic discharge we generate a beam of deadly radiation, you know what I mean! High enough to punch a hole through living tissue."

"An A-Bomb!" Exclaimed Captain Kapil.

"Exactly like an A-Bomb." Madhav said. An A-bomb was a small payload capacity atomic bomb, lower than 10 kilo tons, developed during the third world war to destroy enemy Drones.

Madhav remembered the brilliant light it emitted every time his platoon fired one on the test subjects.

A bunch of crewmen from the Reactor department surrounded them. Madhav saw Reena twitch her fingers as she waited for him to come back.

Madhav enjoyed the attention he got. Ratan tagged along, running his fingers through his hairs. Ratan was explaining Reena and a bunch of girls how Madhav managed to identify the problem.

"What are your plans for the night?" Reena said in her honey voice when a stout man with a streak of grey hairs moved through the group. He was accompanied by a smaller man who had an uncanny resemblance to a mongoose. They walked through as if they didn't exist.

"What's with them?" Madhav asked.

"He's the vice admiral and that's Mahesh, his apprentice." Reena said.

"But that guy was not with us in the institute, was he Rat"

Reena spared a disdainful look before turning back to face Madhav, "He is not an ISRO apprentice like you guys. He is more like his personal pupil. He is a Petty officer but behaves like a Captain."

"The Vice Admiral is powerful, and wealthy." One of the girls said.

"He is the reason for all this crappy food we endure! Everyone knows that." Reena spat.

"If it's so obvious why don't you guys do something about it?" Madhav said.

"He heads the Indian seat at the Rotunda." Shree said crushing her glass of fizz drink, spilling beads of liquid on her fingers.

Madhav understood. He had too much experience with bureaucracy. He knew that a member of the Martian parliament must have powers what they call 'beyond the scope of mortal men'.

"What amazes me is why such a high ranking politician would be on-board!"

Just when things began to look dull, the Admiral walked in and silence fell over the room. All eyes were on him and the crewmen eagerly waited for the night's address. He looked over at him and said in a crisp voice that carried across the room, "Well done boy! Captain Kapil made an excellent choice. And since you trained so hard and got us out of that tight spot, I've decided to promote you to Petty Officer."

One of the girls from Administration held out a medal on a silver tray. The Admiral pinned the medal over his chest amid gales of applaud. The gathering turned into a party before long. After a while, Madhav moved around to the observatory deck on the top floor.

Reena appeared alongside him and entered the observatory. It was a donut shaped room with a huge free space in between, covered by a transparent glass dome. The round gallery lined with portraits of legends. While he observed the glass dome, Reena tripped over him. He shot out his arms and caught her before she hit the floor. A strong whiff of her perfume caught his nostrils. She smiled at him, a wide smile. She had big almond shaped eyes. Madhav straightened and pulled her up. She walked away thanking him. That enigmatic smile still etched on her face. Ratan came jumping in and slapped his back, "You are a hero buddy."

"Will you grow up?"

"She is smitten! I'm telling you! I have a way with girls, believe me she'll do anything for you."

Madhav looked around and saw Shree with disgust etched on her face and move inside.

"Rat! Think before you speak. We are not kids anymore."

"We are craving a relationship and you wanna squander away your chance? God won't forgive you."

"Shut-up!"

That night he dreamed of Reena all over him, seducing him with her voice while Shree watched from a distance. Sulking and angry. Madhav wanted to comfort her but Reena held him. He stretched his arms to touch her. Shree froze at his touch and exploded, burning and spraying hot molten lava all over. Madhav woke up with a start. He tossed around and went back to sleep.

Evenings were the morale boosters from the routine five-hour wormhole haul.

The Captain was a natural when it came to flare up emotions. And he had his methods. One day, he'd talk about the planets he had visited, next day he'd run a bollywood movie on the central screen.

Lieutenant Puneet and the Vice Admiral had war stories to share. Once, they called Petty Officer Shree to share her experiences, but she refused.

Madhav realised this was all a way to keep everyone motivated through endless dark space.

They had their first ever space combat session on day eighth. Madhav sat with Ratan on the seat closest to the door. Reena sat behind him, eying Madhav with interest. The sonorous clank of his feet on the grated metal floor announced the Admiral's arrival. As he entered, the metal reflected the obtuse gathering hall. Madhav had not seen him this close before. He looked exhausted. His puckered face was big with dark shadows underneath the watery eyes. His skin had increased folds, stretching the scar on his forehead. His missing right ear looked like a dog had chewed on it. He somehow looked much older and thinner. Reena was poking Madhav in his ribs when he stomped his robotic limb hard on the floor with a clang. Silence fell.

"I won't waste your time by teaching you team-work and responsibility. If you know that, it's good. If you don't, you die."

There was a general accent of murmur.

"Right then. War - if it ever comes to that, is fought by men. In my regiment, we deliver! No matter what the situation, we deliver! If the missile works, good! If it doesn't we find a way to make it work! It doesn't matter what you think, because the enemy isn't going to let you go. You might have a nine month baby at home waiting for you to return, but the enemy doesn't care.

"Is it true you cut your own leg off Admiral?" A deep voice said from the back of the hall.

Madhav turned. It was Petty Officer Shree, standing close to the exit.

"Yeah! This would be interesting" Ratan said.

The Admiral gave a harsh laugh and sat on one of the tables. "I bet it sounds all heroic, but it wasn't! It was terrible, to be honest."

"You got a metal leg!" yelled Ratan.

A hint of murmur ran around the room.

"You want one, boy?" The Admiral stared at Ratan, who lowered his head.

"This leg can never be like the one I had. It's sluggish, slow and hard to control. Every time I close my eyes, I see is my severed leg laying in a pool of my own blood."

Silence filled the room.

He snorted suddenly!

"I surprised the enemy, hacking through, hopping on one leg."

There was a stunned silence.

He jumped down on his mismatched feet and moved forward. "A strategy is as good as the person who employs it. I was broken and bleeding like the Monsoon Rivers. I had stepped on a land mine and my platoon had moved forward into the enemy lines. We were outnumbered three to one. Our Commanding officer came up with an old strategy. To bluff the enemy into thinking we had more forces. So we decided to spread out. Luck wouldn't have any of it. The explosion lifted me ten feet into the air and I landed on my backpack strapped to my waist. My leg was dangling like a water hose. I wanted to die! The pain! I can never forget the pain!

I wanted to lie down and sleep in the quite hospital wing and watch TV. I had suffered an accident. Wounded in action, my report would read. A medal and a promotion. I'd be a celebrated war veteran even if I choose to lie down there and wait for someone. It was the perfect rationalization.

I knew my body was weak, killed even with feathers, but my mind! My mind was divine! It knew I was capable of carrying out the assault. It knew that I had it in me to endure. I needed to accept it! To accept that I was afraid. As soon as I realised, everything went back to normal. I was at home, the one place where I could be me.

I ripped out the Khurpi from my belt and hacked off my leg. I didn't wait to look at it, stood up and went on!

You know what happened? We were able to push the enemy thirty kilometres behind enemy lines. When backup arrived, we wreaked havoc!"

He stood in the centre of the class, looking into infinity.

"That's when I learned strategy is as good as the men who follow it."

"Perseverance! It's always the last hit of the hammer that break-opens the treasure."

When it was time to leave, a buzz of chatter burst forth.

"He cut his own leg off?" Ratan said.

"Didn't it hurt?" Madhav asked. It seemed incredible to imagine the young admiral hopping on one foot. Carrying his INSAS - bull-pup, amid a torrent of bullets flying on all sides must have been frightening.

That night at dinner, Reena, Ratan and Madhav sat on a table with the standard supply. A fruit, one biscuit, Chapati and cooked vegetable curry. With the daily dose of spirulina tablets. All in vacuum bags on blue Styrofoam trays.

"I don't understand!" Madhav said.

"What?" Reena said, raising her eyes from the plastic plate she held. She was sitting next to Madhav close enough for him to smell her flowery perfume.

"Why did the Government green light this mission?"

Ratan shook his head and sighed, "Not again."

Madhav shook his fist and said, "Can't you see? They are not space explorers, they are soldiers. There is something we don't know."

"'They!' You see yourself as different from the rest of humanity?" It was Shree. She stood over Reena's shoulder with her ration in hand.

"That's not what I meant."

"Don't you know why we left you out alone on Earth?"

"What do you mean?" Madhav yelled. The room went silent. All eyes were on them.

"Why don't you tell everyone who you are, Madhav Sharma?"

"What are you talk-" Madhav protested.

Shree cut across, "They don't know you, but I do. And I bet you wouldn't want that revealed." Shree stomped out throwing away her diner with a soft thud.

"What does she mean?" Said Ratan, holding a half eaten chapati.

Ratan and Reena shook their head in disgust but Madhav knew what she meant. Everything that had happened to him flashed before his eyes. His years of hard work usurped by his partner, the board voting him out. Government black suits seizing his fortunes. He stood up not wanting to eat any more and left Ratan and Reena on the table.

Since the fiasco at the dinner table, Shree never missed an opportunity to insult him. Madhav felt his face flush every time he'd see her.

One day, one of the crewmembers, a famous communication engineer, caught Madhav in the middle of the hall. He requested him to test a new communication device, a thin 8 inch by 4 inch glass sheet. Madhav, bored by the description of the antenna looked around when the yell of his name rescued him.

"Hey Madhav!"

It was the Captain. He waved at him from the far end of the corridor.

"Care for a walk to my cabin? The Engineer of Navigation has a very low view of you, but I'm sure you'd prove her wrong."

"What happened? Did she accuse me of something horrible?" Madhav said.

"She knows who you are."

"I figured!." Madhav sighed, "I know what she thinks I did."

After a pause he added, "It's not a big deal. I've been accused of far worse."

"Worse than blowing up a planet?" He picked-up a slip of paper and read, "Madhav seems to instigate rebellion by asking questions."

"Oh! So it's a thought crime, is it?"

"No no no… don't get me wrong. It's good that you are inquisitive. But you are not permitted to disturb the psychological balance of the crew."

"What kind of a place you've brought me into!" Madhav stopped in his tracks and stood at the entrance of a small cabin. The gate had a plate marked with the Captain's name in gold lettering. He was one of the five. The five who ran the place. The Admiral, Vice Admiral, Captain Kapil, Lieutenant Puneet and Petty Officer Shree.

They entered.

The Captain pointed to a news clipping on his study table. It showed the smoking image of the Kronotsky Volcano. "The Martian colonies of India demand freedom and the United Nations support them. They think we did that on purpose."

"But there are plenty of habitable planets and I'm sure if we can travel through wormholes others can too."

"That's the very reason we have to scavenge for a home planet. Every known habitable planet is claimed. Lunar and the Martian colonies, Proxima-B, TRAPPIST-1, Norio planetary system all claimed. Our prime minister has decided to surrender and dissolve the Union of India. This ship, this seventy five men crew is India."

"We can fight for land! Can't we? We have a massive army…"

"Really! After all that has happened! Wasn't the death toll of the war good enough for you?"

"That's not what I meant!" Madhav mumbled.

"Admiral Ian took up this project from Prime Minister Vajra as a last ditch effort to save the race." There was a very tense pause, "If we fail, India loses."

Madhav bit his lip. If the mission was so crucial, it was even more foolish to recruit untrained men.

He said this to the Captain.

"You forget! The colonies of Mars are no longer Indian. Union of India remains dissolved."

"But these film stars, politicians, public figures, who migrated to Mars this decade? Are they not Indians?"

"In blood, maybe. Not in faith. They demanded a free nation the instant India's involvement in the core experiment came to light."

"Ungrateful pricks!" Madhav spat.

"Or people who have had enough of it!"

"How can you defend them?"

"I'm not defending anyone. All I'm saying is they have a right to live a better life. Let's face it. We have never been good with governance. They got a chance, they took it."

Madhav thought for a moment. If someone had asked him to leave his country and start a new life, he would have done the same.

"So now we either find a planet to set-up our base or die trying?"

"That pretty much sums it up."

That night, he was invited to the crew meeting attended only by the Five. He was talking to an over enthusiastic Reena when Shree walked up to him and handed him a note. It was a square white leaf of office memo that had three words in crisp thin handwriting. Conference hall @ 5. Signed by Lieutenant Puneet- Head of the Engineering.

At five, Madhav entered the conference cabin in the centre of the hull. Within minutes the Admiral barged in. Vice Admiral Yashwant, Captain Kapil, and Lieutenant Puneet followed. They wore the full decorated combat uniform with medals gleaming on their chest. The Admiral's shoulders and shirt pocket looked like a museum for medal display. Madhav noted the highest military honour, the Anant Vir Chakra on his chest. The captain sat immediately next to the Admiral on his right. He too had an array of medals that sagged his shirt pocket. The Vice Admiral sat with his arms folded, with an air of indifference. The admiral directed Lieutenant Puneet to start the meet. The Lieutenant cleared his throat.

"We have received recent images from the TRAPPIST 2 Binary system." He said.

A pixelated image of an orb popped up on the presentation screen. "This is G72, in the habitable zone from the white dwarf. Tiny size, gaseous, looks like no surface to land."

He flicked his screen once more, "This is G73, in the habitable zone from the white dwarf. But all spectral analysis points towards a possible gaseous giant…"

The Admiral slammed his fist on the table.

He yelled, "Is there a point in showing these images if you haven't identified a planet to set base?"

Perplexed, Madhav looked around at everyone. Everyone seemed calm, as if floating away into the void of space was routine.

"What's going on?" he said.

The Admiral glared at him. The Captain gestured him to shut-up.

"I do not understand. We have no clue where to go?" Madhav pressed on.

Shree interjected, "Because you do not know…"

"Shree, he is a crew member. He has every right to know" The Admiral said calmly.

"I would like to know why we are cruising aimlessly in space?"

The Admiral opened his mouth but the Vice Admiral spoke first. "Everyone here follows orders. We are looking for habitable planets while we travel the distance. It's an accepted strategy…"

"Thank you Vice Admiral Yashwant." The Admiral cut short, "Everyone here is a soldier. They don't ask questions, they follow orders. My command is good enough for my men to do what I ask."

"That doesn't answer my question."

"I want us to find a habitable planet, before the People's Republic of Russina claims the one in the TRAPPIST 2. I'd rather fight the third world war again than wait to find the next solar system with a planets in the habitable zone."

That made perfect sense. The Peoples republic of Russiana was the biggest country. With China and Russia joined, they had the most men to spare.

"But I have news…," A crewmember said with a wide grin.

Madhav hadn't noticed him before. He was a tall, dark guy with curly hairs and a thin face.

"There is a planet in the Goldilocks zone. T-786. It equals the size of the Earth and looks like it has land. Although it might be mounds of dust in a weak gravitational field…"

The room went deathly silent. Everyone gazed at the screen. An image of a planet with odd structures zoomed in view. It was half dark and half glowing. A huge white spiral formation could be seen covering half of the planet. As the image expanded, crude shapes came in view.

"Those, I think, are mountains…"

"Or mounds of dust!" demanded the Admiral.

"Maybe…" the crewman stuttered, "That's the best image I could get."

"Brilliant!" The Captain hissed.

The Vice Admiral looked at the Lieutenant from head-to-toe. He said in his drawling voice, "Do you mean to say that you have no confidence in the equipment we supplied?"

"Better quality image needs better probes."

"So you mean that the budget wasn't enough?"

"No! I mean that this is the best… look this here is a planet we can explore. But it needs more than a camera and a data transmitter. It needs a rover."

The Admiral lashed on the crewman like a hungry lion.

"You know our predicament Dr. Mithun. You should have gone for a rover straight away. All you have managed to do is waste lakhs of rupees on a probe which is useless."

"It's not useless." Dr. Mithun rolled his eyes in exasperation. "It gave us everything we need to know."

"But you said you do not know if the planet is habitable!" The Vice Admiral said.

"The planet is habitable, but I need more data to confirm if it is good enough to set-up base. I need a probe."

"Are you out of your mind? Where will we get a rover now?" The Admiral yelled.

"Will a scout mission work?" Madhav stood up and said in a heavy voice.

"If by a scout mission you mean to send a lander and collect data, then yes."

"What do you mean?" The Admiral asked Madhav.

"Sir, the best telescopes will not be able to provide him images of the planet. What we need is a surveyor program. We travel to the planet, send a capsule down on the surface and see if it's habitable. We have nothing to lose."

The Admiral stood up. All eyes were on him. "What you say sounds great, but who would be mad enough to risk a landing without sending a Rover?"

9 EMBRYONIC JOURNEY

The TRAPPIST 2 solar system had a white dwarf star in the centre. The planet, T-786, locked in a synchronous ballet with its sun, looked like a blue and orange marble. It looked a lot closer to its sun than the Earth was. Madhav pointed this out to Dr. Mithun. He said this white dwarf star was tiny compared to the sun.

"-and also cooler, making the Goldilocks zone ranging much closer to the star."

A thin blue glow lit up the planet. There were cloud formations, Blue Ocean and land.

That evening, at the meet of the top five, Madhav and Dr. Mithun presented their plan.

"We can enter the orbit in less than twenty four earth hours."

"Kritikarsh orbit insertion." Madhav clicked a button on his communication device. A flight plan displayed on the screen.

"This is where Navigation team," he pointed at Shree, "needs to turn-on ignition."

"Once we are in orbit, the planet's gravity will do the rest. We slow down at the fourth orbit and enter the transfer orbit." Said Dr. Mithun.

"-and at a height of 815.33 nautical miles, eject the capsule into T-786's atmosphere." Madhav completed the sentence.

He clicked again and the image of a large cylinder displayed on the screen.

"The descent starts with one minute and twenty second course correction. Engine cut-off. Reference alignment with the surface and ignition again until touch-down." Madhav said, "Here is a list of the complete itinerary with time stamp for the Navigation team."

"You will recognize the scout-capsule made for invasions but not fit for experiments. We made vital changes to it and made it a walking science lab. This capsule will give us seismic information, geological data, biological data, atmospheric data. You name it! We got it!" Dr. Mithun added.

"That's all very impressive, but..." the Vice Admiral drawled, "Why don't we land on the surface. We are close enough. We can see this looks good for landing." He said looking over his spectacles as if x-raying the two men in front of him.

"Is this your first ever flight Vice Admiral?" Dr. Mithun spared him a disgusted look.

Madhav cut short the Vice Admiral's retort and said, "I'll answer this sir. We have got one chance. One chance to do this right. If we land without any data and this place turns out to be poisonous for carbon based life-form, we are toast. We won't get no rocket nor propellants to escape the gravity of this planet. Now, if we were to send this capsule and make sure that this place is good enough, we can descent down and set-up base."

"Or we could fly away and search for a new home!" Dr. Mithun said with a grin.

"But there is a catch..." It was the dull voice of Lieutenant Puneet. "We would have to abandon the crewmen on the capsule."

"That's a risk Madhav here is willing to take" The Admiral, Ian Cordoza looked over at him.

Madhav nodded amid a racing heart, "But we need one more crew-member. One who can help with the navigation, communication and other crucial experiments?"

"You can train a crew-member willing to be a part. I'm sure you'll find someone."

The Vice Admiral stood up and said in an indifferent voice, "I need a list of all the equipment you have installed on that capsule you modified." He reached for the door and left without another word to the team.

There was a very pregnant pause. Nobody said a thing. Then Shree shot-up her hand.

"Yes dear?" said the Captain kindly.

"I'd like to volunteer for the capsule crew, Admiral."

"You all right?"

"Yes!" She grunted.

Madhav noted her eyes were moist. His stomach fluttered and he urged to comfort that pretty face. He reached towards her but stopped in midway. The gesture didn't go unnoticed and she snapped, "Touch me and I'll cut your balls off. It's your fault we have to go through all this."

Madhav took a step back at the sudden outburst. "Nobody forced you to volunteer. There's still time. You can go back to enjoy life with the rest of the crew while I risk my ass out there."

"It's your fault we lost millions of lives on Earth. God'll never forgive you for crimes against humanity. You destroy our planet, massacre millions and now you want to play the hero. I won't let you get off Madhav Sharma."

"But I…"

Shree took a step forward and tapped his chest, her nostrils flaring. "You know why I volunteered for the mission? So that I can enjoy watching you die. And if the alien planet doesn't kill you, I will."

She had a mad gleam in her eyes. Madhav saw her whipping out of sight stomping hard on the starship's polished floor. He realized he had no choice and checked the time. He dashed towards the third floor and found Captain Kapil in his cabin. He was chatting with a plump short woman who laughed. He cleared his throat and the captain turned, "Oh hello Madhav!" he said with a grin that compared to a toad's face that had a juicy fly in its mouth. The stout woman edged out of the room.

"Er, I was down in the department with Shree when…" He had no idea what to say and wondered if the Captain knew Shree's rage towards him. He hoped he'd understand without much explanation. That he was already aware of Shree's misunderstanding and would help him in the case. The captain merely stared at him.

"She um, She thinks I'm responsible for the failed core experiment."

The face of the Captain went from red to white in a flash. He slid off the desk and took a step forward.

"You do have a repu-?"

The door behind them burst open. Shree stood there with flaring nostrils. Madhav was staring at her but she refused to look at him.

"What a surprise. Madhav here was talking about you."

Shree was standing very erect. "Then I must wait outside for my turn."

"I'd rather you stayed while we talk." Madhav said with a bravado he wouldn't have dared alone with her.

She spared him a disgusting look before entering. She opened her mouth to speak but before she could, Madhav yelled.

"Tell her Captain, I wasn't the CEO when that experiment went haywire. Heck I wasn't even in the proposing committee. The whole thing was the Government's fault."

"Don't lie to me Mr. Sharma. I know-"

"It's true." The captain said.

There was a swelling silence. Madhav's face stretched into a grin. Shree's face couldn't be more obvious. Stunned, she rounded on the Captain. "You know what happened. And still you believe him? Did he buy you off Captain?"

Madhav saw she was on the verge of tears. "I didn't." He said in a fierce voice. He would have continued but the Captain stared him down.

"Officer Shree, Madhav was not responsible for the accident. He was voted out by the board before this contract. Trust me! He is not what you make out of him."

"So now he is your favourite." Tears streamed down her cheeks. Her voice trembled as she gasped for air.

The Captain looked bewildered. Madhav took control and said, "I chucked me out for opposing this experiment. They hunted me down and made me an outcast. I had to wind down and lay low, hiding on an island on the west coast."

Shree was crying now. Through the tears she said, "I worked on the Migration program for so long hoping to find my brother. For three years! I had hope that one day he'll come. But now I know I'll never see him again. He was the only family I had."

"And your parents?" Madhav asked.

"Dad died in the war of Nicosia. Mom died soon after."

"I'm very sorry for your loss." Madhav said.

The Captain said in a small voice "I knew her Dad. We were in the same platoon. Brave man. He died fighting against an army of thirty to one on the streets of Nicosia, while I followed orders to retreat."

Later that night, Madhav and Shree sat together in the empty common room. Each with a steaming mug of coffee.

"This might be the last coffee we have. Enjoy it while you can." Madhav said.

Shree nodded.

"I always assumed you'd be a strong girl. Like a tomboy…"

"What makes you think I'm not strong?"

"Are you?"

"My father taught me to respect elders. I was nine. My uncle used to come home every Navratri. He groped me. He'd touch me and tell me that was a way of praying. One night he ripped my pants off and forced me to sit on his lap. I bit his nose clean off his face. He howled in pain. Father thought I was too rowdy and sent me to Army school."

"Well… I guess I was wrong."

Shree made an odd face. Something in between a grin and a cry.

"I was in the second year of college when the Great War broke out. I went back home to find mother in shambles. We started a small bakery to get through the dark days. Father never came back. We received a tri-colour coffin. Empty! They never found his body. I enrolled in his stead, and joined on the Himalayan front. There, I met Captain and has been family ever science."

It was a tacit bond that they shared that night. You don't share something that deep with someone and not become friends overnight!

Clang! - The capsule door slammed shut and plunged into total darkness. He sat there strapped to the cushioned seat, Shree sitting beside him on the left.

This is what he hated the most. Waiting in total darkness! Covered in a special suit with an oxygen generator and anti-microbial fabric. A stream of sweat ran down his spine, tingling him all over. He scratched his head with a gloved hand but to no avail. Any minute now, their capsule would lurch out. The suspense would be over in a matter of minutes. Madhav felt the trembling of metal under his feet. The pulley was at work here. They were being lowered into the vacuum chamber. There was a whirring noise and with a click the console came to life. Shree's face glowed blue in the dim light. Batteries online! She looked at the screen with an intense expression.

The capsule jerked with a loud scratching noise and went askew. Madhav instinctively threw out his hand and held on to the chair.

The lights inside the capsule flickered once and turned on. Madhav heard the vacuum pump shut and the rolling of the shutter.

"The doors are open. Any minute now." He said.

He heard the Lieutenant's heavy voice over the radio, "Capsule 22, ready for drop?"

Lieutenant Puneet himself had volunteered for the navigation controls.

"17 seconds" Captain Kapil's cheerful voice echoed through the radio, "Good Luck team."

"Ten Seconds, Brace yourselves."

Madhav started to shiver. He was strapped on the cushioned chair but he shook like a leaf. There were too many steps to go wrong. And each had to be perfect for the next to be successful. A slight error, even a second's delay of the boosters could launch them into space at an insane velocity. Too long and they would slam into the planet. Madhav shuddered. He wanted to give a better farewell to the Captain who, he thought, had given him a new life. With a sinking feeling he realized he hadn't told anyone about Raja. He thought of speaking to the Captain before descent when the radio crackled again.

"Five seconds to drop, four, three, two, one and Launch!"

Whack- and then nothingness. No sound and no gravity. Nothing!

Then with a bang, the capsule gyrated into orbit.

Shree turned on the booster engine and lowered the capsule into the transfer orbit.

"That was smooth" Shree said through the radio.

"We matched the speed of the drop to the planets rotation."

He heard a soft grunt through the open radio. He took it as a thanks.

"Ready for free fall?" Shree asked.

Madhav felt his heart race. He gave her a thumbs up without much thinking.

Turning off the ignition, Shree plunged the capsule into the planet's atmosphere. For a second everything was still.

There was a soft bump and the capsule trembled. Then they fell with tremendous speed. They were falling, tearing through the atmosphere towards the centre of the planet. Madhav felt dizzy as weightlessness made his insides float.

The quantum thermal protection kicked in. A roaring sound blacked out every sound and blasted through his ears like a trumpet. The windows glowed with an eerie orange light streaked with blue. They fell with such speed that he thought Shree forgot to turn on the redaction boosters. But there was no way to confirm. The entry into the atmosphere rendered the radio inactive until the fire died down. They were falling at incredible speed, losing altitude.

Shree flicked the ignition on and turned the capsule upright by complex manoeuvres.

They were now ten thousand feet above the surface. Madhav craned his neck and glimpsed outside through the window. It looked green, like crystallized mosses streaked with silver. Peaks of a hill rose in the distance, separated by a shallow gorge which glimmered white in the brilliant daylight. A glorious sensation filled his whole body. He could have jumped with joy but for the safety belts.

Madhav turned the radio back on and spoke, "Kritikarsh, this is Capsule 22. We are ready for power descent."

"Cap-22 you are GO for power descent. Over."

It was time to land.

Shree commandeered the capsule towards a flat patch of terrain. They flew up across the mountain, over the liquid filled lake and onto a patch of land. They were now a hundred feet above the surface.

They held-on to the altitude. Madhav could see the vegetation violent sway.

Then, with a piercing clang of metal on rock, the capsule touched down.

10 DOWN THE RABBIT HOLE

"Kritikarsh, the Scout has landed." Madhav announced. He heard a soft hooting in the background.

"That must be the Captain."

Shree turned her head. For the first time in the last forty days, she smiled. Madhav's stomach gave a slight flutter at the sight of her. He unstrapped, opened the latch and looked out.

An enormous hill lit by a dim white sun filled the landscape. Smoke was coiling up from the hills in places. Clusters of dark green ferns flocked a few feet away from the capsule. Madhav slid down the ladder and stepped foot on the surface. He slipped and held the ladder for support. The surface seemed wet. He crouched to take a closer look. A thin coat of dark green lichen covered the land. He looked around. Scattered with boulders, the plain curved towards the hills in the distance. The gravity equaled Earth's. His calculation had predicted as much, still it came as a shock. A bunch of thin red barrel-like plants rattled in a breeze. Covered with black flowers, they looked like devil's horns.

"Ready for me to come out?" His radio buzzed with Shree's excited voice.

"It's wet and slippery down here. And make sure not to lock the hatch on your way down."

Shree chuckled. "I'll take care of it."

"That's our home for the next couple of weeks." Madhav added.

"Indeed it is."

Shree jumped out of the door, climbed down the ladder and fell flat on her back.

"I warned you" Madhav jeered while she clambered back up holding the ladder for support.

"Looks like a fine place. Shall I take off my helmet?"

"Not yet. Let's get some readings first."

For the next hour, they busied themselves with setting up the lab.

Madhav set the power bank and a basic shelter for the equipment.. He started to calibrate the machines. Shree who dragged the heavy communication satellite out. She hid it between the devil's horn bushes and walked back to the tent.

"It'll be better if we retreat inside the capsule at nightfall." Madhav suggested, "Who knows what beasts roam about this world."

Shree set up the communication transmitter in one corner of the tent and started to search for a signal.

An audible beep buzzed from the tiny transmitter and died. Shree pressed a button on the mobile receiver and listened. "Communication is up, batteries are down. Let it recharge while we take a look around."

"My oxygen is at 81 percent. Three or four hours before we need a refill." Madhav said checking his vitals on the helmet screen.

"The best way," Shree argued, "is to explore."

"Right! So, we collect samples. Some rocks, plants and any small creature we capture. At night we retreat, analyse and prepare reports."

So they agreed.

The terrain was smooth. Madhav pointed to the cluster of ferns ten feet towards the valley. The dark green ferns swayed in the breeze. As Madhav moved closer, he saw a tiny rodent like creature dash across the grounds. It hid behind another cluster of bushes. Madhav shot towards it. His suit made him clumsy, but he could still see it hiding behind a thick devil's horn. The creature had thin, tiny legs, five in total. But the legs were not what made him awe. It was the crown of eyes over its head. They blinked randomly and before he could get any closer, it skittered deep inside.

Madhav had a sudden inspiration and he started to record his voice.

"Green, snow-capped hills lit by a dim white sun. Unknown gases erupt from deep fissures rising in clouds all around. Clusters of green fronds with bottled plants that look like horns of a beast. A thin dusting of dark green lichen covers the land. Swarms of tiny five-legged animals hide in the bushes. A narrow strip of eyes wraps around their head, giving them a 360-degree vision."

Madhav looked around, curios. There was life on this planet. He itched to pry open the visor and smell in the air, he was sure would be life giving. But he didn't dare! What if the air here was ionic? It would rip apart his lungs in an instant. The air pressure was all-right but the composition of the air here was yet unknown. He noticed the grounds here were not slippery anymore. Moving across, he saw another cluster of plants.

"There are massive flowers in all kinds of colours, sitting atop thick white stems. The plants look juicy. Some kind of airborne creature circles around it."

He moved closer and stopped behind a shiny-black stone. It jutted out of the ground covered in soft lichens.

"A small bird-like thing held aloft by air-bags circle the colourful flowers. Much like the butterflies on Earth. Moving closer, I can see they have a threefold symmetry. They look like a man parachuting down with legs stretched wide apart. Their face resembles a pit bull pup."

He followed one a little bit farther. They had a nest of colourful eggs. The nest sat on the top of a stone turret that rose nine feet above the ground on an otherwise flat terrain.

Madhav explored until he reached the edge of a hill. Tall grass as long as four feet swayed in the air. Suddenly, with a screeching beep, the suit lighted-up like Christmas. He had travelled ten miles, almost sixteen kilometres. No doubt, his oxygen levels had fallen to twenty percent. He etched a large M with his feet and dashed for the capsule.

He reached in ten minutes.

Shree entered few moments later and plugged-in her cylinder to refill.

"There's a river about ten kilometres to the left. Here," She shoved a bottle of the liquid in Madhav's hand, "I got a sample. I bet this air is breathable."

"I guess the same but why risk it. I'll run some tests and we'll know everything before daybreak."

But night never came. The sky went dim and a gigantic cloud rumbled and thundered. Then with a tremendous clamour it started to pour.

It rained hail stones, as big as ping-pong balls. They'd break on hitting the floor and evaporate into mist glowing with an eerie blue flame. Soon the landscape filled with transparent hailstones evaporating in mists. It went on and on.

"The Passover" Madhav sighed.

"The what?" Shree was looking out of the capsule window on her side, the glass fogged by her soft breath.

"The cloud. It floated away. Like the Passover of Lord over Egypt."

"Are you a religious man?" Shree asked.

Madhav noticed the tone of incredulity in her voice.

"I've read a lot but I don't follow one. My father tried to teach me to be a Brahmin. But I didn't learn. He thought I betrayed his faith."

"Why? What's wrong with Hinduism?"

"My mother was Jewish. She raised me on the Torah, my best friend was a Jain. I read the Bible and the Quran, but I learned, it's all hogwash. Legends, fables, creation myths, undying Gods. Imagination has no end. Every saint, Jesus or Buddha, tried to teach compassion and love. None of them claimed divinity. The people pinned that medal on them for being what they were. Men of incredible caliber."

"That's religion!" Shree added in a low voice.

"A drug to justify whatever they wanna do, never mind the prophet." He said strangling an invisible neck.

"But Hinduism is the oldest religion of the world. How can you not follow it?"

"The Vedas provide a way to invoke various forces of nature and please them. It doesn't force anyone to follow a god. Hinduism gives me the choice to be an atheist. Even that belief leads me to god. Life is as it is, here and now. This is the kingdom of god."

"Hinduism is the true religion. The Santa Dharma." Shree added with some dignity.

"You know why Hinduism survived so long? It's the festivals. As a kid you enjoy the sweets, burning crackers, playing with colours. So many festivals, so many rituals. Even if I do not like the idea of a God, I cannot ignore the festivals that go on all year round. We associate auspicious days with them. Day's we associate with good and bad fortune. You cannot override such deep rooted belief system."

"That's it? Religion is festivities and having a good time for you?"

"That's not what I meant. If there is karma and I screw up this life, I'll be reborn and carry out the fruits. It won't be me. It's someone else's problem. I'll be reborn with no memory of what I did and things can go downclear no clear reason. If my conscious allows me to be what you call 'evil', then whatever I do to others is something they deserved. But I get a pot full of bad karma which I'll have to suffer again in my next life. Then I have no reason to be sulky. I deserve what happens to me. I don't need god to make my life better. What will happen will happen. Why bother!"

They sat there in silence looking at the hails falling with loud thuds on the metal capsule. Daylight never receded. The sky went back to blue from orange as the storm clouds passed and the landscape was dazzling again.

Shree looked at twin peaks of the hills in the distance. Then she took a piece of paper and sketched a map of the area she had discovered.

"What is the planet like?" she said etching a river on the plain piece of paper.

"I saw a five legged animal…"

"No, I mean the landscape." Shree added a curved line and a cluster of bushes to her sketch.

"I saw a craggy hill opposite to the sun."

Shree looked intrigued and stared at Madhav.

"And there it is." He drew the paper forward and pencilled two peaks of a hill opposite to the river.

"Oh! And here we are." He made a circle in the middle of the river and the twin peaks. They had landed on a plateau flanked by the river towards the sun and the hills to the other side.

"You think there's intelligent life here?" Shree asked.

Madhav had been thinking the same. There was water on the planet. An active atmosphere, pleasant temperature, different biomes as far as he could judge.

"There is no reason to believe why there shouldn't be."

"Would they have tentacles for limbs, or fangs for teeth?"

"Life evolves with similar features. I would be more surprised if they don't look like us."

"Aliens look like us? Come-on!"

"Why not? If laws of physics do not change throughout the universe, why laws of evolution be any different?"

"That would explain superman" Shree chuckled at her remark.

They slept for a few hours. Halfway through his sleep, Madhav could swear he heard a wolfish howl.

He got up to take a look and to his surprise he saw a white striped creatures as big as a bison. It chewed on the devil horns a few paces away from the capsule. And then it disappeared in a flash, leaving behind a grey blur.

Every few hours, twilight fell and storm clouds covered the sky. Diamonds filled the land with soft blue mist.

Seven and a half hours later, both were ready for the day's mission. They had limited ration. The pressure to finalise the landing site looked like a bared sword.

They send a message to the mothership with updates and turned on the geo-tags. Then Madhav and Shree split up. Madhav left for the grasslands and Shree took to exploring the river.

He turned his recording on.

"Orange and blue fill the eye as the hills rise out of the green moss-covered ground. Frequent rains keep the stones wet and slippery. Once the rocky terrain ends, brown soil starts and a four feet tall grass cover the landscape. In the distance a couple of hills rise. These hills look very old. Broken boulders scatter around the grassland surrounded by the tall grass. An audible hum of winged bugs fill the air. A slight orange tinge of the dwarf sun over the light blue sky..." He looked around. The boulders were not round but jagged. Like cut out from the hills. The straight line ran almost parallel to the edge of the boulder. He ran his hand over the hot rocks and felt the bump under his gloved suit. The ground was wet yet the rocks had a coarse surface.

"The rocks look like cut out from the hills. There is a long array of these cuboid rocks with straight edges."

He went forward and examined another one.

"Some lines are deep, like cut out from a bigger source, I'm going in" - Hark!

There was a sharp scream on his radio.

"Shree? Everything all right?"

There was silence.

He tried again, louder. "Shree, are you all right?"

No answer.

Madhav checked the location signal on his sleeve. The radar blinked with a green dot some nine kilometers away. He dashed across the wet stone as fast as his suit would allow and followed the signal. It took him through a patch of devil horns and into a grove of light orange barked trees. He hesitated and streaked through to reach the other end. Madhav reached a clearing on the banks of a rapid tumbling down the hills. The liquid - water, he was sure, was clear and he could see round pebbles under the two feet deep bed. A hundred meter away, Shree sat on her elbow with arms and legs stretched. As if relaxing on a summer's day on the beach. Something coiled close to her neck, poised and ready to strike. It looked like a serpent. As Madhav charged forward, lifting a boulder, the thing uncoiled and slithered away into the forest. The blue reptile had a thousand hairy legs that carried it out of his boulder's reach in a flash. Shree slumped to the ground and screamed.

"It's all right. The thing is gone, whatever it was."

Shree breathed heavily and looked in the direction of the escaped creature. Her helmet was intact but a button on her suit was open. It released the pressure maintained inside the suit.

"It paralyzed me. I couldn't move. It was like someone in my head talking to me, telling me there is no other glory than to be the food of the Balazac."

"The what?"

"The Balazac. That's what it called itself."

"What else did it say?" Intrigued, Madhav followed it to the grove. This couldn't have been more alien. A creature that had mind control technique.

The small groove had holes in the ground sort of like burrows. He poked around but couldn't find it. Once, he felt something whispering in his ear but it soon abated. Abandoning the chase, he went back to the spot where he left Shree.

"Did you find it?"

"Looks like it disappeared."

"It said it wanted to taste my blood. It said I will not surely die. For it knows that when I let it drink my blood my eyes will be opened, and I will be like God, knowing good and evil."

"And naturally, you sought wisdom."

Shree looked up at him. "Yes."

"That's interesting." He said.

Madhav noticed a glint of the Balazac's saliva on a pebble where it had stood. He picked it up and bottled it.

After waiting a few moments for Shree to recover, Madhav aid, "Let's explore the river."

The river was rife with activity. The liquid flowed with grace and Madhav was pretty sure it was good old water.

It was turbulent enough for life to exist without a struggle. So they followed it downhill. When the rapid slowed down to the level of a still river, they stopped. Here a nest of light green bubble like plants held the water in tight dam like formations. Some fifty such formations broke the stream into pools of water right in the middle of the river. They approached a dam nearest to land. "

Aaaa-" with a sound like escaping air, a cluster of yellow heart shaped creatures burst forth. Madhav jumped.

But Shree touched one of the creatures. It didn't flee. Then she grabbed one and squeezed it hard. It spilled out of her fingers like mud.

"Hey, what are you doing?" Madhav asked.

"Decoy. The real creature escaped."

Madhav observed small pores like sponge on it. Shree pointed to a dam in the middle of the river-pond where a group of tiny blue bodied bat like creatures gleamed. Madhav turned on his recording.

"Groups of spongy animals work together to build intricate dens on still water. They build yellow decoy bodies from special secretions. Cute and heart shaped. I'd like to name them love bats. Dark blue with flecks of gold on their heads. Must be a common to shallow lakes and swamps. The local plant life takes the shape of small light green bubbles."

One thing was clear! The planet was teeming with life.

"There's a permanent storm cloud inside the upper atmosphere. It moves around and covers roughly one fifth of the globe at a time." Dr. Mithun reported.

Was it right to call an alien planet a globe?

"The air has oxygen, methane and water vapour for sure." Madhav said.

"I don't know if-"

"It doesn't look like a carbon planet to me." Madhav said with force. A carbon planet was one with more carbon than oxygen. Dark and dead. But this one was alive! He was sure he could breathe in the air. Dr. Mithun was orbiting high above the planet without any risks. Madhav and Shree risked their lives here.

"Look, let's wait one more day while you run some basic tests on the samples. See if they are not made of anything dangerous to our composition!"

"Ok." Madhav cut-off sullen at the way Dr. Mithun treated him. Like a school boy!

Shree cleaned the anti-gravity solar cells outside. Madhav plugged in the EVA kit and picked up his suit. A bottle slid out of his breast pocket and shattered. Madhav picked up the small pebble rolling around.

"Ouch!" The pebble burnt his hand and he dropped it again! It was still wet with the Balazac's saliva. A small brown patch appeared where the skin touched the saliva of the creature. He applied a bit of Vico all-care cream, picked up the shards of glass. Throwing them into the waste-basket on his way out, he went to Shree.

"We can take off our suits. It makes us clumsy."

"Are you sure?"

"Oh Shree! Don't you see?" Madhav pointed a moving hand towards the hills and the glimmering sun and the bushes. "Life is everywhere. You think we would not be able to survive?"

"But Dr. Mithun has not…"

"Oh Dr. Mithun sounds more like a college faculty and less like a man of science. I bet he copied his thesis from the Internet."

"You must know Dr. Mithun is a genius."

They were some ten foot away from the spaceship. The devil's horn bushes rattled in the wind. Madhav looked at them. In a moment of heated egotism, he turned his radio off and pulled out of the thick padded helmet.

They looked at each other for an instant. And then, Madhav started to retch violently. He bent double clutching his stomach gasping for breath. He heaved large gulps of the alien air but couldn't straighten up. Shree tried to support him but Madhav felt his head swim as his brain burnt. It felt like bubbling hot acid engulfed his head. His nose sprouted a stream of blood as he tried to gulp more air. His nostrils went so dry, they stung. The green hills went black and he keeled over. He fell head first on the slippery rock with a very audible thud.

All those times he could have died and this is how it happens!
Death by chauvinism! For a girl who hates him!
Very suave, Madhav. Very Suave!
Wait! Was he… thinking?
Or was he dead and all this was a natural? The brain shutting down with closure. Like some kind of a Purgatory.

Something heavy sat on his chest.

Neo, the ginger cat. But Neo was dead years ago when Earth was still the only planet he knew.

Something warm filled his lungs.

If this was death then it wasn't so bad after all.

An urge to see God overpowered him. He put all his might and with a scream, he sat up, alive!

Shree was on the capsule floor beside him, her face flushed.

"I was so worried. I thought you were dead and I dragged you in and turned the capsule air on and gave you CPR." She said all that in one breath.

Madhav looked around.

"What happened to you?" Shree said.

"Exhausted, I guess!" Madhav said and slumped back down on the cold metal floor.

Madhav slept out-cold. He snatched glimpses of Shree taking instructions from Dr. Mithun over the radio. Since night never fell, he felt like sleeping through a long day. When he was sure he could lift his head without retching, he got up and looked around. A silvery long cylinder labelled bio-analyser hissed and beeped every few seconds. He took a closer look. A round piece of a red and black rock locked in a furious testing war with the computer, rotated inside.

"Yay, you woke up! How do you feel?"

Madhav turned around. It was Shree. She stood there without the suit.

"I've been better."

Shree smiled with her big eyes more than her lips.

"I'm glad you are up." She said dropping a packet of glucose biscuits with a thud.

"That's our last packet of food." She looked calm. "We tested the rocks here while you were out. They are rich in Iron and nickel. Some magnetic in nature. Dr. Mithun measured a healthy aurora around the planet." She beamed!

"That means we do not need to suit-up anymore!"

"Yes! Come, I gotta show you something."

They dashed out of the capsule without any form of protective cover.

For the first time in years Madhav was out in the sun without the fear of burns. His skin tickled as the warm sunlight touched his hands. It was a welcome relief from the cold Passover every four hours.

Shree took her to the spot they had encountered the Balazac. From there, behind the grove of tall orange leaved trees a vast clearing opened up. She stopped so suddenly Madhav ran into her.

She picked up a brown leathery ball from the ground and gave it to Madhav. He heaved clutching a stitch in his side. He was still weak from the collapse the other day.

"Break the outer shell. Go on!" She urged.

Madhav twisted the fruit hard. It split in two revealing a bright yellow inside that smelled sweet. Madhav's mouth watered as the sharp sweet smell hit his nostrils.

"Eat it. You'll feel better." Shree said.

And it did. As he sank his teeth into the fleshy inside, the juice filled his mouth warming him from the inside. He felt invigorated.

"What is this thing?" he asked smacking his lips.

"It's delicious isn't it? I have a basket full of them back in the capsule."

"It taste like a mix between pineapple and a guava."

"But that's not the only thing I brought you out here for."

She walked deep inside the forest, through the orange and green tree leaves. Twigs snapped under her feet.

"This," she said pointing to the flat copper land, "seems to be the best option for the landing."

"This is perfect." Madhav said. The capsule had landed on a moss covered rocky plateau caught between a rapid and a hill. Finding a plain strip of land for the mothership was crucial.

"The Admiral has green lighted the landing. I'll set-up the beacon and send the signal."

Madhav and Shree looked at each other.

"So, this is it… our new home." Madhav said in a heavy voice. He enjoyed the thrill and now that the mission was on a close, he felt exhausted.

"I guess it is."

He was eying the horizon behind him. The hills in the distance rose against the backdrop of a blue and orange sky. Suddenly, he remembered the straight cuts on the cubical rocks he had seen on the foot of the hill.

"Those rocks..."

"What?" Shree asked.

He told her about the straight cuts, the sharp corners. The complete lack of natural weathering on the rocks also seemed odd!

"I forgot about them when the Balazac attacked! We need to explore!"

"Calm down! All kinds of formation are possible on an alien world. Constant rains and weather do wonders to rock."

"It was not a regular rock. There were dozens of them lying around. They were very straight. Very cuboid!"

"I once saw a turtle shaped rock on Indus Vallis. That doesn't mean turtles roam the Martian surface!" Shree said with a giggle. She hammered the pole position for the five hundredth meter.

Madhav considered her lack of interest, complete pigheadedness. There was something familiar about the rocks and he couldn't point it out. He decided to go back after preparing the landing site.

Madhav and Shree dragged the hefty communication equipment out of the bushes. It was inside a titanium box, padded so that it could withstand a fall of thousand feet. It took two hours to erect the complete thing. They hadn't bothered to hide it this time. Finally, when it was over, Shree typed in the commands. They held hands and together pressed the send button.

Five hundred kilometers above the surface of T-786, a lone LED light blinked in the darkness of the Admiral's cabin.

Spires of black rock loomed in view. The soft sun glinted bright as the duo crossed the dusty path of ground to reach the foot of the steep hills. The twin-peaks looked menacing up-close. Boulders and weathered rocks sprawled all across the ground. Small tufts of acid green grass relieved the bleak harsh view. Madhav heaved as the path became steeper and steeper. Shree strode ahead, her feet holding on to the notches in the rock. As they reached closer, the air became colder. Madhav pulled his shirt closer and wished he had the exploration EVA suit on.

"There!" Madhav exclaimed and rushed to a cuboid shaped boulder, almost three feet in height. He bent on his knee and started to examine.

Shree sat beside him and ran her hand over the grooves.

Madhav pointed out the other dozen or so boulders, all with the same marking. Two deep straight grooves, parallel to the edge, running the perimeter of the rocks. Some of the rocks had broken corners but most were similar in size and, Madhav guessed, weight.

"They look exactly the same." Shree said.

The air was full of an eerie whistle made by the wind escaping the cave.

"Do you think we must go inside?"

"It's dark. We'd need a flash-light." Madhav said.

Shree pulled out a couple of diode torches from her fanny-pack and tossed one towards him, "Here! Let's go!"

Inside, the cave glittered as light bounced off the slimy walls. A hint of a sharp pungent smell lingered in the air. A soft whisper, like wind sweeping a drying cloth ate at Madhav's ear. He screwed up his eyes and looked for the source. The cave wasn't too deep and a fissure at the end of the tunnel looked like the source of all the commotion.

"It's annoying!" Madhav yelled.

"What's annoying?" Shree said.

Madhav strained to hear her amid all the raucous the wind escaping the fissure made.

"This sound!"

Shree shrugged as if it didn't bother her.

Suddenly, Shree gave a high pitch hoot and moved closer to the fissure. "Look here!" She said.

Madhav moved closer timidly, fearing the sound would intensify. But it didn't. And then he saw it. Right above the fissure a shape etched on stone. He strained his neck up to take a better look. An inverted Y without the tail with a small circle inscribed in its shadow.

Madhav didn't know what to say. He looked at Shree. They stood there like two art historians ogling over a fresh discovery of cave paintings.

"We," Madhav said in a strained voice, "are not alone!"

As soon as he said those words, the whispering boosted to maddening heights. It pierced his ears and stabbed the back of his head, throbbing.

Little lights erupted in his eyes as he tried to staunch the pain. Even Shree screamed. A terrifying scream. Madhav forced his eyes open and immediately wished it was a dream. Five blue eyed men with golden locks looked down over them. They wore green skirts over a thick green vest, clutching a long rod that buzzed with a dancing blue spark at the tip. Another man came out of the fissure which had enlarged to the size of a doorway. He was in a white toga. He made a strange guttural noise and pointed to the blue sticks. The men followed him in a flash and poked them with the ends of their sticks. An electric pain shot up in his body and rested in his brain. His head felt leaden and within seconds, everything went dark.

11 RAIN WHEN I DIE

Madhav jerked his eyes open. A dull throbbing right behind his eyes made him to squint. It was dark but he could make out a coarse stone chamber, sort of a dungeon. He tried to move but failed. A rusty old metal ring sort of like a Ferris wheel pegged him to the stone wall. He hung in a horrible travesty of the Vitruvian man. A guard sat at the doorway wearing a headband that projected a blue veil over his eyes. He turned his head and, looking over at him, gave a harsh cry. Footsteps echoed in the corridor and three men entered through the giant doorway. They looked like the epitome of blue eyed Aryans Adolf Hitler might have idolized. White, tall and with golden hairs, they wore dark green loin cloth under a thick vest made up of flat one inch stings. A pointy spear end peeked out of a wooden shield holstered on their skirt.

Madhav commanded, "Release me!"

The men ignored him. They pointed at his eyes and etched something on a thin white slab. They were talking to each other. Ignoring a struggling Madhav, the men or whatever they were, kept etching on their white slab. A minute passed in which Madhav screamed twice and tried to free himself with all force. One of the men came closer and pried open his jaw with the stone pen he used as a stylus. The other noted something down in his slab of white tablet.

The guard stood up and once again screeched in that strange tongue. Seconds later, another blue eyed alien entered. The man had a chiselled frame. His sculpted muscles visible through the thin white toga supported by a shoulder pin. For shoes he wore wooden sandals that made loud clattering noise when he walked. The men dropped their casual manners and made way for this newcomer. He came closer and looked at Madhav who felt his face flush.

"Release me! We come here in peace." He made his voice as deep as he could.

The alien grinned and looked at him from all sides. They jeered, making shrill remarks and pointing at his face. Madhav felt a surge of energy and put all his might in breaking away the thin cords holding him. It dug deeper into his skin, tearing into his flesh. A drop of blood appeared on his right hand wrist and trickled on his forearm.

The Alien stopped so abruptly, the other two walked straight into him. He stared at the drop of blood racing down Madhav's arm. Then, as suddenly as he had stopped, he stretched out a finger and touched the thick red bulb of blood. He lifted it close to his eyes.

"Blud!" He said, mesmerized.

The two men beside him gasped.

A crazy possibility appeared to him. What if these men were some ethnic East European tribe who had left Earth long ago?

While the man kept staring at him wide eyed, he screamed again, "Cut me loose!"

It worked, or so he thought. The alien took a step back and for a second Madhav thought he would release him. But then, he disappeared behind the table and returned holding a metallic helmet. Only, it had spikes all around it.

One of the guards worked a lever and lowered Madhav. The iron chains rattled and clanged against the metal wheel.

Madhav gaged as he pushed it down his neck without the slightest concern. With a soft click all went dark. And silent.

Then with a flash, a searing pain erupted in his head. An electrifying pulse shot through every nerve in his body and his brain went on fire. He wanted to scream but couldn't. His life started to roll in front of him like an old Technicolor movie. From his birth to his days in college. His agitation against climate change, ousting from the board of directors. His last night on earth. The news of the failed core experiment, his escape, destruction of earth. Everything!

Madhav thought he was dead. And yet again, and to his utter surprise, he could see. The shooting pain up and down his spine stopped. But a dull throbbing still grilled his back. They snatched the helmet off and connected it to the headband of their leader. A holographic screen projected out and curved over his eyes. There was silence for a full minute punctured only by Madhav's groans.

A minute later the leader took it off. A drop of what could only be sweat appeared over his pale white forehead.

Then he spoke. And Madhav could understand him.

"They come from a different rock of a different star!" he said.

It was like a button turned on and he could make out what they said.

"Master needs to see this!" The Alien continued.

"They destroyed their planet and now they have come for ours. The sons and daughters of Brahma have come to destroy our planet" He said hysterically.

"But sire…"

"Shut up!" He howled. He looked quite insane, spit flying out of his red lips eyes as red as blood.

He rushed out of the room and the two followed in his wake. The clatter of wood over stone faded away in the distance.

In their haste, they hadn't raised his scaffolding back. Madhav looked around. The handcuffs looked like made up of some thin flexible rope attached to a much larger metal chain. The chain passed through an array of pulleys. The room had a stone chair without any armrests. Its centre faded in symmetry that bore the marks of years of sitting through. Behind it, a small mound of soft yellow dry grass served as a bed. The guard sat motionless, the blue screen clasped over his eyes.

Madhav thought. Lowering him had left a gap behind him with the wall. He could swing but to what end? Everything here was stone. A stone table in front with a few levers and pulleys that operated the scaffolding. It was in all probability a torture machine. He was glad the Aliens were soft on him. They took him to be one of their own at first. But then, when he saw blood on his arm, he took out the helmet. He forced the metal ring to swing and struck the table with a loud clang. The table did not budge. But the guard sat bolt upright. He smacked Madhav hard with a wooden baton and went back to enjoying the blue screen.

His limbs burnt with fatigue and he felt parched. He yelled at the guard but he sat there motionless, the blue screen slapped around his face. Infuriated, Madhav swung with all his might. With a mighty crash of metal over stone, the rusty wheel broke and Madhav was free. The Guard bounced on his feet but before he could lift his baton, Madhav pounced on him. With a volley of curses he rammed his head with his fists. He punched him twice and then three more times with a satisfying thud to make sure he was down for good. He then took his baton. It was heavy for its size but the wood was smooth. He peeped out into the corridor and found no one. A strong smell of ammonia rented the air. There was a gate at the end of the alley but the individual cells had no doors. There were eight cells and he was in the seventh. The opposite wall was bleak and there was a dim light entering through a tiny square window at the wall at the dead end. The cell had no doors or grill, instead they had holes on the two sides. Madhav worked a lever outside the cell and rods appeared out of the holes. He closed the cell at the last cell found Shree tied to the round scaffold. He freed her without thinking about the raucous he made.

"Did you see?" Shree said, terrified. Her thin hands trembled and Madhav could hear her heart pounding.

"Let's get out of here first!"

"Where are we?" Shree asked.

He instinctively looked at his wrist band. It was gone! He looked over at Shree's waist and sure enough, her bag wasn't there. They were bare foot with only their clothes in place.

Madhav looked out of the small window. "We are high up in the twin-peaks."

They rushed towards the only doorway left for escape.

Shree dashed towards the exit but Madhav stopped her! "No! Stop! There are no guards here. There must be something to stop us." His voice echoed down the hall.

"Something like?" Shree said.

"I don't know. Booby traps? Lasers? Giant fire breathing dragons?" Madhav said. The aliens had some weird piece of technology!

"Maybe it's activated by touch."

He touched the floor. Nothing happened!

He extended his hand and hit the floor hard.

Nothing.

"There's nothing here. Let's go!" Shree said.

No! Wait!"

He went back in the cell and worked the lever that creaked. He dragged the unconscious guard out of the cell and carried him out towards the door.

"Wait! What if he dies?" Shree asked.

"Better than us!" he said and took position. With the might of a prize-fighter, he thrust him out. A gigantic slab of dark rock came down thundering and slammed on the floor with a crash. The hall trembled with the impact and drowned their Shree's scream of horror.

It rose up without making any noise. A paste of pink mass and bone in a pool of red blood dripping from the rising slab of granite lay there.

Shree spared a quick look before covering her face. "Yuck!" She said.

"Barbarians." Madhav spat. His voice shook with terror.

They crossed the hall reached a staircase.

"There's no one here." Shree said peeking around.

Hope and courage kept them moving. The fort had a putrid smell of decay. Figures of lotus and men carrying triangular flags covered the walls. They avoided the dark corridors and kept looking for exits. They entered a hall that looked like the one they escaped. Their blood chilled at the sight of rusty triangular seats. A lever operated cartwheel soot in the corner. The stone walls were dead cold. Thin shafts lighted the stairs and they descended in absolute silence. The staircase got narrower and terminated into a solid wall. They stood there in silence. Their hearts pounded in their throats. Then, Madhav stretched his hand and touched the rough wall. He found a loose stone. He pressed it but nothing happened. He pressed harder. Unyielding, the stone remained impassive. As a last ditch, he put his whole body behind it. The stone whirred and rotated halfway. The boulders began to shift. Soon a hole large enough for them to slip out, opened up in the wall. They jumped out and found another pillared hallway. Larger and loftier!

Giant rock cut pillars made the hall look like a durbar. The ornamental figures with four hands and three heads looked familiar to him.

"Doesn't it remind you of the Elephanta Caves in Mumbai?"

"I was right, wasn't I?" He exclaimed. His voice boomed in the stone hall.

"Right about what?"

"Those rocks! Look at the nose of that dancer there. That three headed thing! Look at its eyes. So alive."

In his excitement, he had forgot they were prisoners of an Alien tribe.

He examined the stone pillars, the exquisitely cut figures and the polished stone pedestal.

"We must warn the Admiral!" Madhav said as the pain shot back again in his spine and brought him back to reality.

At the end of the hallway, they found the fissure they had been examining before the abduction.

"I'm curious," Shree said as they encountered no one on their way out, "Why was there no one to guard us!"

"This looks like an abandoned fortress. Or a prison. What intrigues me more is the sculptures were hindu Gods!"

"You think they are humans?"

"They have blood and bones like us."

They were running across the grasslands now. Not having his wrist band made him feel like he had lost a vital part of his body.

"I don't know what time it is." He said.

"We spent four hours inside that fort."

"How can you say?"

"The rains. It happens every four hours."

They reached the bush of devil's horn and Shree rushed forward

"They took the capsule!" Madhav said, horrified.

They stared at a patch of green mouldy rock. Patches of brown visible where the capsule had burnt the mosses while landing.

"Where the…" Shree screamed a word she had never used before. "What do we do now?"

They rushed to the landing site but the satellite and communication equipment was gone.

Madhav stood there. The clock was ticking. There was no time to think.

"We need go get our stuff back."

"Back where?"

"To the fort!"

"I say let's hide. Let the Kritikarsh land. We can meet their leader and resolve this once everyone's here. If we go now they'll kill us."

"If we do not warn the Admiral they might ambush and kill every last person on that ship!"

Madhav could see he wasn't making sense to her. But he had understood what the Alien said. And he was afraid to admit he could understand them.

He felt unclean, like infected by a deadly parasite that might harm everyone around him.

"You stay here! I'll go get the communication equipment."

"No!" Shree said stomping her foot. "You'd die! Besides, you don't even know where they took all our equipment."

"Why is it so important to warn the Admiral?" Shree asked as they traversed through the tall grass. They had made a canopy out of tree leaves to save themselves from the hailstones. The clatter of the hail felt like the static of his old television.

"If I can talk to their leader and explain thing-" He said fending off against a bug that tried to sting his face.

Through the grasslands, they reached the base of the hills. They took cover behind a black stone spire and peeped towards the cavern. A dozen green skirted stood guard. A red skirted alien was squawking instructions to the group.

"He is briefing them on our appearance…"

"How do you know?" Shree looked at him amazed.

"I'll explain later."

He strained what the guard said against the hails on stone. The echo was better and he could catch most of it.

"Oh! For God's sake! We are fugitives for murder and treason. They want to take us to the city of Egomyard" Madhav spat raising his arms in exasperation.

"Not off to a very bright start for foreign relations" Shree said.

One of the green skirted guards raised his hand. Their commander turned to him and his voice echoed down the hills.

"He asks if we have fire sticks. The leader says we have something far more sinister."

The leader, at that point, pulled out a dirty and stained bag. He held it like forward and dropped it on the floor.

There was an audible gasp of terror.

Then he said something.

"He thinks we are from Bacaim with terrible weapons and a false god who justify killing innocents. Well well!"

Madhav sighed. "They have a council meeting in the city of Egomyard!"

"Let's go to their city and find out our stuff."

"I must go alone from here! You wait for the admiral at the landing site!"

"No. I don't get it! Why are you making this worse? If they catch us, we die!" She seemed more than a little excited.

Madhav thought for a moment and slumped down on the ground with his back resting on the black spire.

"When they used the metal helmet on me…"

"What metal helmet?"

"They made me wear a spiked helmet and extracted my memories" Madhav said.

"Did it hurt?"

Madhav dismissed her with a sarcastic smile and continued.

"They saw us destroying the earth and escaping, colonizing mars…"

Shree's eyes widened, "They think we are invaders!"

"And we help cement their belief by killing their guard"

Shree formed double quotes with her fingers and flexing them twice, she said "*Accidently* killing their guard"

Madhav peered over his shoulder and slumped back.

"The quickest way to get back to our equipment is if I surrender. They take me to their city. You follow and get back our equipment."

Shree went a shade paler. "How will you escape? The ship arrives after two Passovers"

"They are like us. Flesh and Bone. I'm sure I'll manage something. But you need to send that message. If you fail, everyone dies!"

"No! She said, "I'll come with you. We are in this together."

"You have the training and the experience. I'm a loser! It doesn't matter if I die. Do what I-" hark!

But he could not complete the sentence, for at that instant, he heard the buzz of something electric close to his neck. He knew even before he heard the harsh voice, they were discovered.

The one advantage Madhav had over these medieval beings was that he understood them. But they seemed to know this and used their batons and hit him hard whenever he said something. He braced himself but they were hard hitters, professional and cruel. When they looked satisfied with his screams of mercy, they bound them tight and hurled them into a wagon. The strange white-striped beast Madhav had seen grazing pulled the wagon.

"They do not hurt me! They understand I'm a woman." Shree said.

She seemed to enjoy this which infuriated him even more.

"They are like us." He said.

"Everyone can see that-"

"Like their civilization, culture, it seems I'm back on Earth."

They travelled at breath-taking speed. Past the craggy summits and the grasslands, they reached what looked like the edge of a medieval town. Large meadow with small huts. People raking the fields, smoke through thatched roofed chimneys. Soon, they entered the city. Madhav saw a tight cluster of red bricked houses, none higher than two floors, with tapered roofs. Laundered clothes dried in the air, children played in the mud. The chatter on the street infected Madhav. Intrigued, he scooched to the window for a better look. It looked like a medieval city. Dirty and crowded.

Then a sight flooded him with relief! The capsule towered over the shambled huts. It was moving! Close to a whitewashed building next to a bridge. He kicked Shree in the shins. The gushing noise of flowing water rose over the babble of crowd and the putter of the wagon.

Few moments later, they stopped. It was in the middle of a market. The two guards jostled and thrust them face down on the dusty path. They raised their electric sticks and Madhav closed his eyes fearing another attack. His legs were still burning. A crowd had gathered all around them. He turned to see a square with a lone black stone obelisk in the centre. It had queer markings etched on it. Madhav thought this was a public execution. But there was no scaffolding. Or a guillotine. So hanging and beheading were out. What then? Stoning? A preferred method of execution drawing large crowds. Yes! That was it!

Madhav waited in dread of the fate reserved for them. Shree looked at her feet and seemed lost.

Then, a hooded man came forward. He stood in the centre of the podium and took off his cloak. Silence fell!

The man was six feet, with a giant body. He could have been a fine wrestler were he on Earth, but here he looked more like a general. His golden locks tied above his head held by a band of orange leaves. A metal chain glinted on his right wrist. He opened his arms wide and spoke in a deep voice. Madhav had to strain to hear what he said!

"Men of Canneti! A crisis arose in our city which have brought about destructive consequences for the Republic. The council of elders are unable to prove their worth. And they label my conquest as the end of democracy. They dishonour our republic. For betrayers and informers the dungeons is the proper place. The lies which veil us from our misfortune must stop. The fraud of the present council must be exposed. That will stiffen your necks. I, in the command of my elder son Shax, have captured the biggest threat to our existence. These two murdered the chief of my personal guard and escaped the dungeons. They have called upon a greater number of their species to annihilate us and capture our towns. I have seen what they are capable of! These menial beings! Dregs of existence, ruled their planet with fear and repression. They warred amongst themselves, killed millions of their own and exhausted their planet of all its riches. Now they have come here to destroy us! These Earthlings have unleashed this war against the People of Egomyard, while the council fattens its purse! I have been standing by and observing the situation for sixteen rains now. I have issued warnings repeatedly. And I have intensified these warnings of late. But the council watched on.

And now I have lost a brother!

My son lost a mentor!

And you have lost a fierce warrior.

Did he deserve this fate?"

The crowd erupted into a hellish encore. "No!" They cried.

He raised his hand and silence fell once again. People listened with rapt attention, every word their leader said!

"Suspend the council" Someone screamed through the silence.

He gave a lopsided grin and spread his hands. "I, Beelzebub, son of Rahzebub, proclaim myself the ruler of Canneti."

The crowd went berserk! Echoes of Victory to Beelzebub erupted all through the square.

The red skirts held their spears high and ululated. The mob was starting to gain a life of its own. Everyone fixated on their new leader and for a second, Shree and Madhav stood there forgotten.

Suddenly, a yellow skirted guard fired at Beelzebub, missing him by an inch. The other guards lunged on him. Some more revolted. A fight broke out. Members of the crowd panicked. In the confusion, the guards engaged the rebels in a skirmish.

That's when he took his chance. As the mob mobilized, Madhav stage dived and crashed over two of the red skirts. He snatched their fire sticks. The attack and the ongoing pandemonium gave him the crucial seconds he needed to burn away his ropes. Shree joined in and kicked the two hard on their face. They ran into the crowd. They shoved and pushed and with a herculean effort, reached the edge where the crowd thinned. The sky had turned grey and the first hails stones were already hissing close to their feet, rising up in a blue mist. Madhav put all the juice he had left in his legs to run. His limbs felt independent of his body, neither stopping, nor caring! He reached a fork in the road and saw the capsule on the right, reflecting the grey clouds.

He didn't slow down! He rushed through the cluster of shacks and reached the foot of a stone bridge. The Capsule, propped up on a wooden scaffold attached with wheels, stood there. It swayed as four guards pushed it. They stopped to look at the intruder.

Right then, he felt a sharp pain over his chest. Something hit him hard like a bullet and he lost balance. The fire sticks flew away on the pathway with a clatter. His face smacked the stone and his nose shattered. Blood filled his mouth sickeningly and dripped into the muddy puddle on the street. A hard kick to his ribs mad him cry in pain. He spit out a mouthful of blood and turned. A red skirt was standing over him, holding out a fire stick that smoked at the end.

When the final orbit before power descent started, the Admiral grew curious. He had been in fifty evacuation missions, taxiing this spacecraft from the Indian evacuation base to the Martian colonies. But this was different. This was an Earth-like planet. And they had been afloat in space for far too long. But all this was trivial. He was excited because he was the one on whom the onus of keeping the race alive, rested. He would have laughed, if a year ago someone suggested that he'd be the saviour of the Indian people.

He had been a patriot as far as he could tell. He helped his friends, killed a lot of bad guys for the government. And when the revolution came, he joined the forces. Then the war broke out. Five years and an economic collapse later, the supreme leader had to step down. And down came the men who had supported him. The loss of life had been so high, it was a miracle he had survived albeit with one leg. Supreme leader had been ruthless in his working. But the new government was kinder to its people. He got a medal for his command in the European front. He was promoted to Brigadier, and given a bionic upgrade. He also got a desk job. He soon missed the fronts. The sights he had seen, the things he had done, they were not for the faint hearted. A coup d'état was not what he was willing to do, although he considered it several times. He knew his men would die for him as they did for Napoleon. But this was not the 1800's and he was no Napoleon. Then the right opportunity arrived. There was an opening in the DSA, short for Defense Space Agency and he applied. It was still early days of space warfare. India after a five year Great War, revolution and tyranny of thirteen years, considered upgrading its technology. Brigadier Ian was promoted to Admiral Ian and given charge of the office. Nothing but true faith in his Country could have given him the strength to reform the department torn apart by years of neglect and vast embezzlements. The department functioned on a secret constitution drafted in 1999, eighty one years ago. It was so outdated that the first time he read it, he took it as a school project of his secretary's nine year old.

He set up a drafting committee rewrote the entire warfare strategy. He introduced capsule infiltration, probe espionage, rover warfare and other space-war strategies.

When the UN came running in to save the world after the great floods he came back from retirement. He led a team of seventy five and in forty days evacuated 24 Crore people to the Martian refugee base.

After the failed core experiment, the prime minister fled to the lunar colonies. So did his cabinet. His disappearance led the Martian colonies of India to increase agitation. They demanded total Independence. Which they did with surprising speed owing to the fact that most of them were high profile citizens. The common man was either stranded on a dying planet, or left to rot on the Martian base. The UN and other world leaders distanced themselves from India.

The Admiral couldn't stand the injustice, and called forth his old team. He took charge for four hours, making him the shortest Prime Minister to hold office.

A light on his desk glowed and brought him back. It was an incoming message from Petty Officer Shree. He pushed the button and listened.

A high pitched voice of a sobbing woman rambled through the phone. "Admiral, it a trap! Do not Land! It's a trap."

He could hear terrible screams in the background. He also heard a strange crackling that sounded like fire!

He picked up the phone and yelled into the receiver, "What do you mean ambush? What's going on! Update your location!"

But the line went dead.

Then the announcement speaker buzzed, "Power descent initiated. Drop in fifteen seconds."

The Admiral hastily dialled the Engineering department and screamed, "No! Stall the landing. Stall it now!"

"But sir, we have shut off the engine. We free fall in five seconds."

And before the Admiral could retaliate, all motion stopped. For a second, the ship floated in mid orbit, and then with a wheeze, dropped. There was nothing he could do!

The red skirted man held Madhav down with his boot while a bunch of yellow skirts ganged up on Shree. She had reached the capsule before him and had one hand over the speaker. The communication panel was a couple of paces away. The capsule rested on a three feet high scaffold on wheels. Rest of their stuff lay bundled beside the metal tower. All Madhav needed was a minute long diversion and Shree would be able to send a warning light to the Admiral. With the kind of experience he had, he'd know what to do. In all the roaring of the riots he had to yell to share his plan with Shree. The red skirt didn't find it funny and hit him again with the blue spark. Little lights erupted in his eyes. He felt like his head would burst open.

"Leave him" Shree screamed, sobbing.

Madhav tried to get up with his hands outstretched. The air was full of deafening explosions. Amid all these, Madhav could hear the soft licking of water behind the Capsule. A crazy idea got hold of him. The red skirt wavered his fire stick but Madhav looked at him calmly, hands in the air. He spoke in a slow manner and made hand gestures as if the guards were dim-witted. He pointed his finger to Shree and said "Let her go."

He moved two of his fingers imitating a walk.

"I" he pointed to his chest, "Will surrender." He raised his hands, palms facing the red skirt.

To Shree he added rapidly, "Call the Admiral as soon as I hit him. Don't waste even a second." waving his hands in cross to throw off the yellow skirts.

The riots seemed to be abating as cheers of Beelzebub came crashing down the street. They were close to the stone bridge where Madhav and

Shree were stranded. The mob gave a loud cheer and Madhav took his chance. He ran head first into the red skirt and rammed him into the ground. The gang of four pounced on him. But survival instinct kicked in and Madhav dashed across the bridge. He moved towards the capsule, thinking of nothing.

He was inches away from the latch. He didn't know where Shree went but he hoped she made the call. The latch was a foot away. His fingers brushed the cold metal but he needed a few more inches. He put-in all his might to grab it when an explosion shook the ground. Madhav felt a punch hit him in the guts. He was thrown across the bridge with an almighty force. The world turned upside down and he fell across the stone arch, into the river. With an angry splash, icy cold water rushed into his ears, mouth and nostrils. He tried to swim but his limbs were too heavy. Quite suddenly, he felt as though a hand choked his throat. He made a valiant effort to swim but couldn't move a limb. The water was so cold, it felt like a glacier. He struggled for breath and gulped a mouthful of muddy water that made his head spin. His eyes stung and his lungs went empty. He fell down into the river and hit a rock. He floated inches from the river bed, flowing with the current.

His will gave way and he let go, wishing it would all end.

He wanted to rest. Let other men take charge!

12 THE WAR OF CANNETI

The ground exploded and hurled Shree off the bridge. She fell face first into the centre of the muddy street, splashing dirty water all around. Four yellow skirted aliens held up a large long barrel that looked like a canon, smoking at the ends. Madhav was not in sight. The intoxicated mob, men in shabby clocks, marched down the street like wild elephants. The ululating reverberated around her as she regained her senses. The smell of singed skin was nauseating yet she lay there hoping for someone to pick her. The four yellow skirts and their commander leaned over the bridge looking down. The capsule wasn't standing anymore. It had crashed over a cluster of shacks under the bridge. And judging by the screams, someone was injured. Shree wasn't sure she ought to be thankful or sorry. She mustered every inch of her strength and got up on two legs. Following the muddy path, she ran through the claustrophobic shacks. Snaking in and out through the cobbled streets run-over with muck. She zipped past a two storey building where a bunch of guards stabbed a man in a white toga, who howled in pain. Some of the shacks were burning. People screamed and children cried. Another elderly man was being beaten up by a gang of yellow skirt solders and a robed man. She couldn't take it anymore. She rushed into the cluster and rammed the one in centre. Taken by surprise, the other attackers moved back as she hurled a fury of punches on the one she'd landed. Then she smashed his head on the stone street with all her might. With a sickening thud, blood sprouted from the alien's nose and he lay motionless on the street. One of the three yelled something as if challenging her to fight. Shree, her bloodlust unquenched, turned around to look at him. It was the smallest of the group, five feet eleven, still a foot taller than her. But she was not alone. The aged man also stood beside her with a dagger in hand. The three fled.

Shree stripped the fallen alien off his robes and donned it. The cloth was coarse and smelled of old books and decay.

"Satsta!" the old man bowed to her.

Shree bowed too. The old man pointed towards the centre of the city and said breathlessly, "fsi cha!" He gestured her to follow and started to walk, "Shaa ho."

It didn't take the smarter part of her brain to understand that the old man asked her to follow. They were both the fugitives and Shree was pretty sure, an enemy of the enemy was a friend.

She embraced the dank robe closer as the Passover receded. Four hours from now, her friends would land.

Or would they!

What if they never land? That was part of the deal wasn't it? That's what they had signed up for! Favourable, they land! Unfavourable, they flee!

If that were true she imagined how the Admiral would respond. He'd call a meeting. The Vice Admiral wouldn't advice risking his precious ship! Dr. Mithun would want evidence and ask for funds to analyse the threat. The Captain would ask everyone to reason but end up supporting whatever the Admiral says! It would be the Admiral then, who'd decide. And the crew's safety would be the one thing on his mind.

But she couldn't risk it! She couldn't let Madhav's sacrifice go in vain. He was arrogant, yes. And a pig! But he had risked his life. He was brave enough to make sure the race lived on. She wished someone would wake her up and it would all be a dream! But she was a realist! And as realists go, she had to make most of the situation she had landed in.

The old man turned a corner into a narrow street. Shree rushed behind him and stepped into a pool of brown water. The alleyway smelled like rotten eggs. She clasped a hand over her nose and followed. He walked briskly, stepping over the puddles, grabbing his toga above his ankles. He stopped in front of a wall covered in moss. It was a small space between two buildings with sloping roofs. It was a bit cleaner here than the rest of the street. He looked over his shoulder and pushed a square stone brick in the wall. It parted from the one adjacent and a slice opened up in the solid stone wall. It was so thin, Shree had to turn sideways to enter, as did the old man. The slice collapsed as soon as she entered and they plunged into darkness. First time since they had landed on the planet, Shree experienced such absolute dark.

The old man yelled, "Ospii spaa kmii."

There was a pop and the room filled with yellow light. Shree covered her eyes instinctively. Then the room appeared out of the brightness. It was a low-ceilinged, square room. It was empty except for a carved four feet cabinet in the corner. In the other corner a small glass ball floated in mid-air. Inside it, a fire crackled lighting the room. A young man in red skirt stood there barefoot. He glanced at the old man and looking at his bloody ruptured face, rushed forward.

They spoke in their tongue. The younger one had the same chin and the resemblance was uncanny. The old man pointed towards Shree a couple of times. Finally, the young one came forward and wrung her hand, speaking what seemed words of thanks to her.

"Satsta! Satsta!"

Shree again pointed to her lips and said, "I don't speak your language."

He nodded and pulled out a white headband. Shree had seen the guard at the twin peak wearing one of these.

As she slapped it across her forehead, the red skirted man tapped it and a red light flashed twice. The red skirted man had one on too.

He said, "Shu nini Rahab."

The screen beeped and a translation sounded in her ears, "My name is Rahab"

"I'm Shree" She answered.

"What language are you speaking? I do not understand you. Where do you come from?"

"She is from Earth! Beelzebub wants to kill them!" The old man joined in with a band across his bruised forehead.

"From Earth! Then we will have to synch our schema. We will need the helmet of Bor."

They escorted her to an inside room and sat down on soft cushioned settees. Everything was exquisitely carved and gave an ambiance of Royalty. The old man had a pin with an inverted Y without a tail and a circle in its centre. It was the same symbol on the fissure at the twin peaks.

The young man reappeared holding a helmet with spikes. Shree remembered Madhav talking about something similar. She hesitated. What if it was a trap? But then the bruises on the older one looked real. Also, she had murdered one of their guards in front of this old man. Maybe, this was the way to communicate. Indeed, Madhav had started to understand their speech.

She timidly put it on. A rainbow of colours erupted inside the helmet. Blue sparks danced all around her eyes. A fiery red lasso of light zoomed inside and hit the blue sparks. A shower of red and green stars rained down on her. And then it went dark again.

"Power Descent initiated!" The voice of Captain Kapil floated into the microphone. The Admiral sat there clutching the cold metal of the chair as hard as possible. The quantum shield had deflated, and the ship was ready to land in next ten minutes. There was nothing the Admiral could do when he received the cryptic message from Shree amid sounds of raging fire and chaos. He peeped out of the window and saw dense foliage towards the left and a hill with two peaks to the right. The landing site reflected the laser sensor and locked the area marked for landing. It was close to a river, in the middle of a clearing next to the jungle.

The quantum drive that absorbed the heat at entry into the atmosphere had exhausted. It could, if reversed, have been used as a defensive wall against any attack, nuclear or explosives. The admiral didn't get time to either brief or prepare the team for an attack. Once they were four hundred feet above the ground, he scanned the entire area for any sign of an enemy he had no idea about. If the message was to be believed, and which he did for Shree was not a crew-member who'd lie, there was an enemy in ambush.

There was only one way he could imagine for survival. He took to the microphone and pressed the button to speak, but before he could say anything the speaker buzzed to life.

"Kritikarsh ready for touchdown, Admiral."

The Admiral took a deep breath and said, "Kill the engine!"
With an almighty crash, the biggest spaceship humans had ever made, landed on T-786.

Rahab pulled out the helmet and asked, "Are you all right?"

Shree could understand him. His words sounded strange but she knew the meaning.

"Did it work? Can you understand her?" The old man nagged from behind.

"Say something." Rahab said gently. He was leaning over her chair holding the armrest so tight, his fingers turned pale. He was still wearing the helmet and so was his father.

"I can understand you." The hard k's and s's made her realize she was speaking in a different language.

Rahab smiled and fell back on his chair.

"What just happened?" Shree asked leaning forward.

"The helmet of Bor synchronizes your schema with ours. We can speak Hindi, Marathi and English. And you can now speak Shii. Now tell us who you are." Rahab said.

"I'm a human! From Earth! Our planet was destroyed…"

"So it's true?" Rahab screamed. Eligor recoiled and gave her a look of utter discomfort.

"We come here in peace. We are not here to conquer your cities." Shree said quickly looking at the terrified faces of the two.

"We heard that story. You drilled deep into your planet and ended up exploding it. We do not travel in space. We cannot risk a species as destructive as you to land. Your forefathers were ousted from our planet for being too violent. And today, you return after exhausting everything you had." Eligor said.

"What do you mean 'ousted'?" Shree jumped on her seat.

"You don't know?" Rahab said, "They don't know" he added to his father.

The elder one, Eligor, pulled out a book from the cabinet next to him.

"This," he said, brandishing an old gold lettered book in front of Shree, "is the Sukshm Veda."

"Veda? Like the religious book of the Hindus?"

"The helmet of Bor tells me that you have different social and cultural systems of belief for a being you call God! Hinduism is one of those systems." He said more to his father than to her.

Eligor closed his eyes and sat there in silence, the helmet still there on his head, glowing slightly.

Then he spoke.

"Millions of years ago, when the universe formed, the first conscious being made this planet. He gave birth to Brahma, the all father. Also known as Odin, Elohim, Adam and many other names. He created sixteen sons and one daughter. They lived here in harmony for many years. They spread out over the planet and increased in number. Everything was good for a time. Then, one day the one of the tribes made out a sculpture from stone and dedicated it to the all-father. Another tribe created a shrine for him where he could be worshiped. They put the sculpture and seated it in the shrine to worship, thus forming a super-tribe. Soon the two started to fight over whose work was superior. The fight escalated and soon a war broke out. The devastation was such that the other fourteen tribes, who lived peacefully, complained to the all-father. The All-father ruled that they both were his creation and he couldn't take sides. They were both right. The fourteen tribes then went to the first conscious being. The first being on watching the destruction and loss of life, lost his temper. He banished the two tribes to the third planet of a young sun in a different galaxy. He cut off the all-fathers fifth head and exiled him. He cursed that he would never be prayed by his own children whom he let die. They left Canneti, taking with them all the technological advances and arts. They took all architects, engineers and doctors. Canneti was left with politicians and schemers. That's why Canneti ha no art or technological advance."

"God? Brahma? The fifth Veda? What are you talking about?"

"Yes! And we are his children."

"Seems like a pathetic excuse to hide the governments inefficiencies." Shree said with a disdained look, "You believe everything written in there?"

Eligor snorted, "I never expected you to believe. Your tribe has been in exile for so long, they don't know what to believe anymore. Jesus, Allah, Vishnu, Buddha and a thousand others. So much faith in your shamans, in your pundits. All revealed truth."

"It doesn't matter what your holy book says. We are not here to fight!"

"Then there's no reason for us to go to war!" Rahab said calmly.

"Yes there is!" A deep voice said behind her. Shree turned and saw a face that made her cold with terror. She felt stupid, lured into a trap. On the doorway stood Shax, the son of Beelzebub.

The gigantic ship stood there like a mountain. It's all eleven doors were marked. Catapults with spiked iron balls, eight hundred kilograms each were ready to be fired. The stubborn and strong-willed Beleth had always dreamed of a conquest that would gain him the favour of his brother, the King. Beleth had commanded many a army against the Bacaim's, but this would be different.

As a commander of the free city of Egomyard, he had twelve victories against the continent. It was a huge number, surpassed only by twenty five victories of the King's son Shax. But as the king's brother, this was his first chance. And the King had given him a very important task. To annihilate the intruders. These filthy looters had already leached their planet. And now they wanted to exploit Canneti. He wondered why the first being allowed such people to happen. Turning back to the war at hand, he waited. He waited for the ugly vehicle to open its doors. He imagined the raids, the shower of burning arrows, the siege tower demolishing the roof of the vehicle. The dwellers inside screaming in terror as the armies of Beleth stripped them of every ounce they owned. But then a nagging doubt fell over him. What if they just fly away the way they came? This was something none of them had ever encountered. And the strategy he followed was a simple one. Simple but effective! No attack without surprise!

One of his generals came riding a striped aakii that flew at the speed of speech.

"You have a message Sire" the General said, bowing down to him.

"Who's?" Beleth asked. He did not like to talk. His voice sounded as though his larynx was scratched.

"Prince Shax! He asks for an immediate meeting."

Shax had always been a threat to Beleth. Beelzebub's favourite son and a better general, he was the natural choice to the throne. A throne Beelzebub and Beleth had dreamed for together in their youth. They had planned elaborate Coupes, fiery speeches and promised the awakening of the race. They had worked at it slowly, year after year. They lost, bribed officials, but never succeeded in taking back their father's crown. But when the earthling's came and that moron councilman termed them as the lost tribes, instead of making it a warm homecoming, they decimated the council. Such was the genius of his brother. The timing couldn't have been better. He was sure Shax would speak of some elaborate scheme and ask favours but Beleth was tired of it all. This was his battle and his glory. Even the twenty five victories of Shax were due to his training.

"Not now" he answered in his scratched voice.

The general knew better and left him in peace. His master was notorious for killing his generals. His temper knew no bounds and his wrath meant gruesome death.

Shax's letter changed the equation. He couldn't deny the prince his meeting. But attacking now would mean losing the element of surprise. He wanted to massacre the humans as soon as they opened the gates.

In a haste, he gave the orders to attack.

Marching in towards the ship, the archers dug in their bow and fired. A rain of fire arrows bloated out the sun as they descended on the gigantic ship. Bouncing off the metal body and the glasses, it hardly did any damage.

Beleth went on with the arrow attack for five rounds barely scratching the paint off the vehicle. Enraged, he ordered a full scale invasion. All the siege towers and all the catapults were to be closed in.

He wanted Beelzebub and the people of Canneti to remember his name, Beleth - Slayer of the human race!

The Admiral and the five members of his inner circle sat there watching the rain of arrows.

"Barbarians" The Admiral screamed.

"What do we do Admiral? We won't hold much longer. We do not have unlimited food." The captain said.

The Admiral grunted. He knew if they opened the gates it would be hunting season for these barbarians.

Then suddenly, Lieutenant Puneet attracted his attention to the radar screen.

Catapults, Siege equipment's, battering rams came closer to all the eleven gates of the spacecraft.

The Admiral stood up and called upon all the seventy two crew members in the common hall.

"Comrades, we have been surrounded by an alien barbaric race that wants to kill us all. If we do not open the gates, they will burn it down. But if we open the gates we will die in combat. We have two choices before us. We either surrender or be taken as prisoners and executed. Or we go out of that door and surrender!"

The crew heard him in silence.

"We have three converted Atomic bomb guns and twenty plasma guns."

The gate opened!

The humans came charging out of the spacecraft. The ground was wet and soon the area where they landed looked like a quagmire. The humans floundered in the mud as wave after wave of fire arrows came crashing down the sky. Some stuck in the mud perished easily. Some impaled themselves accidentally over exposed arrows. Soon, a giant ball of iron came crashing through. Bodies flying everywhere, the crew men bolted in all directions. Dismay and confusion unnerved everyone. The Vice Admiral and Mahesh behind him, raised hands. They identified the commander and raising shields made from the metal of the ship, marched towards the garrison. The ground was wet and slippery. Giant metal balls crashed beside them with thuds and sometimes the blood curdling cries of one of their mates. At last, after a walk through endless pit of mud and bodies, they saw a tall man on an ornate wagon and fell straight at his feet, begging for mercy. The crew, or whatever remained of it, surrendered!

In a single file, men with raised hands waded through the mud, now churned into a thick paste of blood and earth, and dropped at the wagon of the alien commander.

Admiral Ian looked out of the small window. The Captain and the Lieutenant covered him as he waited for the Vice Admiral's signal. They had entrusted the Vice Admiral to save as many lives as he could. And he did very well. The Admiral had expected a total annihilation. His only chance, as Vice Admiral Yashwant had suggested, was sabotage. The two races looked eerily alike. They could seep inside their ranks and slowly rescue the surrendered prisoners.

It they could escape death penalty that is. The Vice Admiral boldly came forward and took the onus to save the crew from such violation.

"But, only you can drive an espionage mission, Ian." Vice Admiral Yashwant said, "You'll need young spies. Take the Captain and the Lieutenant with you."

"And how would we escape?" The Captain asked.

"Wait for my signal."

The Vice Admiral and the crew stood in front of the enemy with caked mud on their boots. They raised their hands in unison and dropped to their knees.

"That's the signal." said the Admiral, remembering the same tactic used by their enemy once during the great-war, a personal joke between the two veterans.

The Admiral, the Captain and the Lieutenant used the eleventh door and slipped inside the jungle. A dozen guards clad in red skirt, gave pursuit. The Admiral was reluctant to use an A-bomb and all three had picked up a plasma gun. Once inside the forest, the three split and took attacking positions over tree tops. They entered the forest and waited. Inside them, revenge raised its hood like an enraged monster.

Everything was peculiarly quite. Soft trickle of water broke the stillness around and reverberated on the thick tree trunks and grey boulders. A drowsy dream like mist hung low over the forest as the sun died. The Admiral camouflaged with the thick groves and waited. The guards entered the forest, howling, mocking, and calling them names. So loud were they that even the laziest of the beasts roared with anger. The humans became possessed of the dominant spirit of the spirit of the jungle and in the three hours that followed, butchered every single one of them. The three then made a lair in the forest. Now it was time for retribution.

13 STAIRWAY TO HEAVEN

Madhav floated face down on the still water. Twisted shapes of different colours danced in the dim light. Something black streaked past his eye. Its head flecked with streaks of gold. A minute later, he realized that he was lying on a bed of pebbles. Small, round stones pressed against his body. He closed his eyes and with great effort, flipped over and gulped a lung full of air. The endless swish of a wave against his head made him aware of his body. He decide to open his eyes again. He was intrigued if he would be able to see the sky. Light dazzled him and he put up his arm to save his eyes. Gradually vision returned and he could see again. He lay under a bright blue sky, with a slight mist. He turned to see the lake but it was half hidden by the fog. His ribs shivered in the icy wind. He sat up. He touched his stomach. A sharp pain ran up his chest and he yelped. Then, a whisper reached him through the unfathomable mist surrounding him. A soft whisper that intrigued him. It was like a voice, kind but grave. Much like the voice he liked to imagine he had. It echoed so close, he jumped, sure to find it behind him. The whisper was louder now. Calling him closer! He whipped around as a breeze ruffled his hairs. His heart drummed fanatically against his chest. The whisper got louder and louder with each passing second until it became unbearable. He clasped his arms over his ears and, like a giant ostrich buried his head in the sand. He had hoped that the whispering would stop instead it became deafening! Madhav got up and bolted away from the lapping ocean caring not where he went. The insistent buzz in his head seemed to lower. He went deeper into the woods. The ground became steeper and difficult to tread. He walked on. The run made him thirsty. He kept his eyes open for a drink. The forest had given way to a mountain. The breeze was fierce and cold. Madhav wished he had more clothes. He was wet and the cold air cut his skin like a knife. His cheeks burnt from the frosty winds.

He looked around and heard the rhythmic pop of bubbling water. The sound came from inside a small opening in the mountain a few yards away. He entered to find a pool of hot spring water surrounded by an orange bush. Soft steam issued from the pond. He dipped his hand. The warm water soothed his cold skin. He gulped a handful and washed his hands and feet. A patch of sticky mud held on to his feet. He looked around and saw a stick some ten feet away near a thorny bush. He bent down to pick it up. With a sudden whipping sound, the Balazac, posing like a harmless tree branch, hissed and slithered inside the bush. This gave Madhav such a fright, took a step back and slumped on the ground. Then he heard it again. That deep, kind voice that reverberated through his heart.

"Madhav", it said, "Son of Abja. You have come a long way."

Madhav turned around. He was sure he was alone, yet the sound seemed to come from the bushes.

"Don't be afraid."

"Who's there?" He asked timidly. Beads of sweat appeared across his forehead amid the cold breeze. His heart hammered against his chest and he felt dizzy.

"I am your God! And the God of everyone else!"

He spun around. A man sat on a stone dais, wearing nothing but a red and yellow skirt. His legs were folded and eyes closed. An aura of tranquillity radiated from his half closed eyes. Madhav could think of nothing, could smell nothing. All he could feel was an invisible power surrounding him, the source sitting in front of him.

"Come closer. Sit next to me."

Madhav, afraid he might offend him, covered his face with his hands and sank down on his knees.

"Rise, Madhav, Son of Abja, who descents from Shandilya son of Brahma. I have given you my protection. Death has returned and you must go back and finish the war you have started."

He opened his eyes and looked up at God.

"My hands are weak, my mind is shattered. My body quivers at the gentlest touch. How am I going to fight these barbarians with fire spitting canons and electric guns? What is the glory in killing someone else and stealing their land? My desire to win has lost!"

"You'll allow them to kill? These people clouded by greed? These, who see no evil in killing someone in their bid to power?"

"It's their part of karma, their sin. They who kill and deceive men for the pleasures of kingdom."

"And how does karma repay them? Answer me Madhav, haven't you experienced karma?"

Madhav sat silent. He wanted to say karma repays in the next birth but he kept mum.

"Karma repays with fate. Whatever happens, happens within the laws of nature. If you experienced pain, someone caused it. And your deeds become experiences of others. These creatures you so easily abandoned, they depend on a higher experience through your action. Do not deny them their fate by running away from your true calling."

"O Lord! I am not as enlightened as you are. I saw these people. They are like me. Like us on earth, yet they do not understand us. We are proclaimed as enemy. And you say my deeds will shepherd them to a higher realm?

"Why do you ask HOW? And WHY? Why don't you perform? Listen to your heart and give us what we deserve. By not performing your duties, you deny everyone the fruits of your labour. Let me decide the fruit. You put in your effort."

"Enlighten me, O great one! How do I listen to my heart? How did you come into being? And how do you know all this?"

"I am the first conscious being! I was aware! And I accumulated enough energy to create! Fields affecting fields! Energies and forces being created! That's how I created the universe, and everything within it!"

"But you look so much like us. Even the tribes here look like you."

"They are my sons and daughters. I gave them my seed." He said all this without moving his lips. "It is I who speaks in your hear! It is I who tells you what to do. When you imagine yourself doing something you might do better than someone, it is I who has inspired you to do so. "

"Then why do we find it so hard to listen to our hearts?"

"Because like me another being gained awareness in the void. I accumulated while he dissipated. I created and he destroyed. Thus the cycle of creation and destruction kept the universe alive. When you are distracted from your goal, when you are caught in the web of lies that you believe to be your reality, when everyone around you deters you from listening to your true calling, HE is at work. He pulls you away from me and shoves you on the path of destruction."

"But what can be gained by destroying a mere life on a tiny planet in the vastness of universe?"

"Things you do when you listen to your heart, brings the entire race a step closer to me. You accumulate your genius and build upon it, inching closer to the thing that created you. When you listen to your heart, you contribute to that accumulation of genius. When you are distracted from your true calling, your soul fails in its mission. The mission to discover the creative genius it was meant to be. Your soul has to journey back in the mortal world to contribute to the awakening and until it does, the cycle of birth and rebirth continues."

"Why do we have an increasing population? Doesn't it contradict what you say?"

"I keep creating new souls. Just like the stars are endless, just like the droplets of water are infinite, so is the creative pursuit. I cannot stop creating and HE cannot stop destroying!"

"But HE destroyed an entire planet and millions of souls with it!"

"It has happened before and will happen again, infinitely. Your world will be reformed again in a few thousand years, life will be reborn. A new species will roam the world that was once yours. I cannot stop creation and neither can he stop destruction. So I use him creatively. We are the Asura and the Devas, the Yin and Yang, Vishnu and Shiva. Our cosmic dance keeps the ocean of universal creation churning."

"I never believed in God. Why are you revealing all this to me?"

"Because you listen to your heart and did what was destined for you to do. Your atheist belief system freed you from any rigmarole and with it the fear of god. You do not help the needy because god is watching. You do it because you feel its right. And by listening to your heart, you inch closer to me than any priest or shaman ever will."

"O great one, show me the way! Tell me whom should I defeat and whom should I save?"

"Do what feels right to you, without the fear of God! Perform your duties and you'll never need my guidance. I might be around though."

And with that he extended his arm and touched Madhav in the middle of his eyes.

With a brilliant light everything disappeared. Madhav was back on the ocean beach, water lapping on his face.

14 BACK IN BLACK

Beleth was beside himself. In a quarter of a day, he had captured sixty nine prisoners of war, losing only fifteen of his men. The humans, earthlings as they were now termed by the new King, were not so frightening after all. Not for him, the great Beleth, Master of Earthlings. He marched the prisoners to the halls of solace on the twin peaks for safekeeping. He could meet Shax there! But first news of his victory was to be sent to the King. He called for a messenger but was interrupted by a guard. It was one of Shax. That impudent little prince! He didn't want to meet him now! But there seemed to be no choice! A moment later, Shax entered his tent.

"Congratulations uncle! What a victory. You'll be served with the highest honour."

"Huh!" he grunted!

"Sixty nine prisoners and fifteen casualties. It seems even the unarmed killed your forces with ease."

Beleth turned around! His eyes turned red. He said in a forced calm, "The humans are brave and fierce. Fight them to know them."

"Ah! Yes! You philosophy of Warfare! Um, there is a certain prisoner of war I'm interested in. I would like to have him handed over to me to be put to death."

"Who is he?"

"Their commander and his band of merry men." Shax said in an off handed way, making himself seem better informed.

Beleth took him to the caravan ready to move. They moved in and out of the queue several times but couldn't find the admiral. Shax reported two more missing.

"Tut tut, uncle! I thought you had a decisive victory over these vermin. Alas, I'll have to find their commander and kill him."

Madhav reached the port of Egomyard through a battered old boat filled with green potato like fruit. The merchant allowed him to travel if he helped unload the sacks at the port.

"Will you sell it in the market?"

"It's for the annual fair and it happens every rain," he said, "but this one is special. They have a new King. Ha!"

At the port, a gang of shabby kids with running noses haggled the cargo laden ships for labour.

A heady smell of garlic from a red powdery substance piled nearby choked his nostrils. He began to unload the quarry as promised. The sacks were heavy. Although he was fatigued by the experiences of the last two days, or eight rains as the Cannetians called it, he managed to empty the loader boat.

His filthy clothes left no distinction between the city dwellers and him. Still, he picked up an empty sack and covered his head. He unstuck his sweaty shirt from his skin and hurried outside the port. He wanted to escape the merchant who was looking for a free slave like him. Inside, the stone city had transformed into silk. Red and Yellow tents propped up in every nook and corner. Some adjacent to the front wall of their huts, some inside the patio of buildings with wooden ladders to the second floor. A tangy smell of fruits mixed with spices hung in the air. He couldn't help when he heard the sound of meat sizzling in oil and begged for one. The stall had a kind lady in black robes frying thin slices of something pink on the spitfire. A little girl inside cleaned the dishes that clinked against a metal basket. Whatever animal the lady offered, it was delicious. It was soft and as he bit into it, the juicy meat and the sauce of exotic spices made him forget the pain in his chest from the fire stick.

Now that he was fed, he thanked the woman who was more than happy to help for it was the coronation of their new King. "Nobody Cannetiya will starve on such a glorious day!" she said in a peculiar rasping voice.

Madhav looked around! Women walked slowly, weighed down by baskets full of vegetables. The stalls were all manned by either children or women. The men were busy in settling accounts, inspecting the decorations and such. Further down the lane he saw a check post where men queued and paid their toll. A soldier in yellow skirt kept an eye out through a looking glass from a tower twenty feet high. Madhav bowed his head and moved on.

He walked against the throng of people going towards the fair. Hundreds of wagons filled with fresh farm produce lined the streets. People haggled with the guards in yellow skirts, haggling with a fistful of glass marbles, Madhav assumed was money.

He kept to the main street looking out for familiar architecture. A building with an arrow pointing upward and an ellipse with a cross in-between appeared. He remembered seeing it and moved on. Further down the lane, he saw the right turn towards the square and knowing the way out, took the left. He prayed more than he hoped for the Admiral to have stalled landing. But there was only one way to know. He walked to the edge of the city following the twin peaks visible over the horizon. There, he stole an akki, the white striped beast with incredible speed.

The instant he sat on the bison like furry animal, everything went fuzzy. All he could see was what appeared immediately in front. It was much like riding a horse, but judging direction was difficult. Madhav estimated that they travelled near ninety kilometres an hour. He kept his focus on the twin peaks and managed to guide the akki through the farmlands. It didn't falter even a step through the changing landscape. He rode it to all the way to the site of the landing. Down the craggy hills and the grasslands. Across the moss covered plateau and behind the thick groove of trees. Right at the edge of the dense forest. Exactly where the nightmare started. He didn't have to look around much. Covered by the towering trees, lay the sixty feet high monstrosity. At first he felt happy, then as he entered the grove, a stab of terror overpowered him. The outer walls lay distorted where the spiked iron balls had smashed. The glass viewer's gallery at the eighth floor looked like a dislodged tooth of a dead animal. Shards of glass lay scattered like snow on the muddy ground below. But what horrified him the most was the bodies. Impaled and shot some hung mid fall in a shower of arrows. It was as if modern humans were no match for these medieval beasts. Madhav anchored the akki and strode through carefully, to avoid slipping in the blood. He could see the first gate, the main gate to the hull where supplies were stationed. He walked slow but recoiled immediately. The lustreless eyes of Dr. Mithun stared at him through a half-eaten skull. An arrow had gone through it, spattering his brains right at the steps of the gate. He bowed down and pulled his boots out and put them on. He took his coat and then tore his name tag from his shirt and pocketed it. Horrified at the fact that he wore the coat and boots of an old comrade, Madhav entered. The insides had been burnt down. Glass crunched under his boots as he went deeper, through the hull and into the main control tower. The barbarians had missed this room. Madhav climbed the grated steps and entered the cabin. There he turned on the central screen and activated the tracers. A round green screen with name tags appeared. He could see Dr. Mithun close to the centre of the screen. A tag named Ratan displayed at the bottom left. Other familiar names appeared. A mound of names displayed far to the lower right corner. Madhav assumed these were the prisoners. Sure enough, his and Shree's name tag appeared amongst the mound. But the tag he had been looking for didn't appear until a dot moved in the top left. It was the Admiral's. His heart hammered! Was the Admiral alive? Two other dots moved. The Captain and Lieutenant Puneet. Madhav couldn't believe what he saw! Was this the opening he needed? A soft drizzle announced the second rains of the day bouncing off the metal sheets above. The three dots began to move close to Ratan's stationary dot, somewhere around Gate number eleven! That was the place where the Balazac had attacked Shree!

There were two possibilities he could think of.

The guards had put-on their suits and frolicked in the dense forests of Canneti. Either this, or the Admiral, the Captain and the Lieutenant were alive, moving towards the mothership. But first, he had to be sure!

15 FOR WHOM THE BELL TOLLS

"What's it like?" The Admiral asked the out-of-breath Lieutenant. Being the younger one, the Admiral had assigned him to survey the settlements of the enemy.

"Well, they are as Shree put it in her message, 'still in the dark ages'! Here."

He flattened a piece of parchment that had a map of the city etched out by a rudimentary chalk made from clay.

"Here's the main square. This H shaped building is the former seat of the republic. Some elite houses then the slums. Here are two stone bridges over the river. The far end has ports and open grounds. A fair has been organised celebrating the new King's coronation." He said.

"Oh! And this building here is where they have jailed the prisoners." He added pointing to the top right corner of the map.

The Admiral patted his back. What the boy had done was no easy feat. Infiltrating an enemy such as this required quick learning and a sharp wit.

"What you have achieved tells me we will win this war." The Admiral said.

The Lieutenant straitened stiff and held out his hand. The Admiral shook it warmly.

"Well done!" Said the Captain.

A message earlier that day had taken the three by surprise. A strange white striped animal had delivered it much like a crow in medieval times. A parchment attached to its leg. The Captain had rushed to the Admiral, thinking it some kind of alien subpoena. At first, the Admiral was afraid to approach the animal, grazing silently in front of the three. Then, after a wait of about three minutes, the Lieutenant lost his patience and snatched the letter from the animal's hoofed legs.

To the trio's surprise it was in Hindi! A letter from Shree wanting to meet after two rains, whatever that meant! She stated that the people on this planet needed help and that the Earthlings could bring it with the right alliance. She said they would be waiting at the edge of the forest next to the river right behind the mothership.

The Admiral, amid protest from the Captain and the Lieutenant, had sent a reply back with the animal.

"It could only be Shree who'd call the Kritikarsh, mothership." He said.

"Still, we must be prepared for an ambush!" the Captain suggested. And so it was resolved that the Admiral will go alone and the two will keep distance, ready with the lighting guns in response to an attack.

The Admiral reached the edge of the forest, at a place where the trees clustered and suddenly opened into the calm river. It was twilight, or so it seemed. The Passover clouds were receding giving the effect of a red sun about to die. It was dark enough for the Admiral and he missed the flash light he kept in his regular cargo pants. But the Captain needed it more. If it turned out to be an ambush then they'd flee and try to survive by seeping into the city as refugees or slaves. They had ample local clothes, money, trinkets and information that would help them.

The captain and the lieutenant seemed certain that the letter was a ploy. But the Admiral thought unlikely,

The Admiral entered the grove. Fragrant fruits made his mouth water, but he dare not eat lest it killed him. They were on an Alien planet after all. As soon as he came out, he saw flickering shadows and heard the crackling of burning twigs.

Was Shree a fool? An open fire that could be seen from miles away? It had to be an ambush.

He walked on!

He could make out three silhouettes, two tall wearing togas and one small wearing a robe that covered its head.

He still had chance to about turn and run! As he thought so, the tallest of the three turned to look and saw him.

"Ah! Admiral" Said the tallest of the group, a golden haired giant in a strange accent.

"Satsta! Admiral Cordoza!" Another of the toga wearing one said.

The third one rushed forward and wrung his hand. The soft touch on his calloused skin let him know who this was.

The girl threw back her hood and revealed a face with a mole under her chin.

"Shree!" he said in an undertone.

"Admiral!" She said!

"What's going on? Where's Madhav!"

"That's why we are here. We need to find him!" She turned around and spoke in a strange tongue. It sounded harsh and cruel with hard k's and long s's.

The one who had greeted the Admiral pulled out a helmet out of a bag on the saddle of that strange white striped creature.

"Wait! Where are the other two?"

"You know?" The Admiral was surprised. "And why are we meeting with a big ass fire right in the middle of an open land that can be seen from miles away?"

"You'll understand! We need to synchronise our schema first."

"Synchronise the what?"

"The schema. Your understanding of the world! It's like experiencing the world from your perspective. It'll allow us all to communicate quickly. But first, you must call the other two."

"You're pretty damn sure this is not a cockamamie bull-shit ploy to kill every last one of us?"

Shree spared a disdainful look before urging him again, "Call them Admiral!"

The Admiral sighed and taking out a thin cylindrical object, sent a second long, narrow and green beam of light into the forest. Within seconds he received two bursts of green light.

"They are coming."

The two reached fifteen minutes later, laden with lighting guns. The Lieutenant walked bare chested, flexing his muscles. The Captain walked beside him, equally charming. Their bodies glowed in the orange fire as they walked into the open from the dark grove of trees.

After a brief discussion where she told the story of her dramatic escape from the clutches of Beelzebub, Shree convinced the two.

"This is Rahab, son of Eligor! Member of the council! And this is Shax, son of King Beelzebub! The council was overthrown-"

"Ahem!" Shax cleared his throat.

Shree looked up, "Oh! He will take away from here."

They were all seated round the fire. It was still dark and the two Cannetians acted as though they were on a regular visit to the riverside.

"Our last king, Leafar faced a rebellion from the peasants. He was forced to abdicate to my grandfather, King Beelzebub's father Rahzebub or Lakim-III. But he was a terrible King. He dealt the rebellion with an iron fist, killing anyone he suspected."

Rahab snorted! "My father was also arrested-" Shax glared at him and he stopped mid-sentence.

"His reign didn't last long. People wanted change! They wanted freedom! Advancement and education. One day, the rebels stormed the gates of our fort and executed the King. There was a mock jury but it was all fixed. Monarchy was abolished! There was a council now. A democratic council and an elected body of governors. People thought that this will improve their condition!"

"But they couldn't run the country, try as they might!" Rahab said chuckling.

"There were rebellions, attacks from enemy states, and a growing sense of foreboding for killing a King! My father offered military services to the council, waiting for the opportune moment to strike! And it arrived with you landing in the abandoned city of Abeesreb! The council decided to spy you and start discussion! But uncle Beleth, younger brother of King Beelzebub, had other plans. Uncle ordered me to capture you and extract

information! What I saw inside your friend's head scared me! I showed him-
"

"Showed him?" The Admiral asked.

"With the helmet of Bor," he pointed towards the helmets he wore, "You can extract thoughts and view it at your leisure." He closed his eyes for a second and the helmet glowed. He spoke again, "like a television broadcast.'

The Admiral nodded. Shax continued, "My father used the image of your planet's destruction to scare the army and with one stroke, reinstated the monarchy."

"That's an intriguing story, but I don't see why you are telling us this?" A familiar voice echoed amid the group.

Shree jumped from her seat and hugged the man. The Captain and the Lieutenant stood u and the Admiral, with his glowing bionic leg, grinned like a child.

"Madhav! You're alive!"

"How did you know we were here?" Asked the Admiral.

"What happened to your stomach?" Asked the Captain.

"I was thrown into the river by that bolt of electricity your men fired," he said pointing at Shax, "washed up on a beach. Had a peculiar dream about a man with a blue neck and came back to see if the mothership had landed."

"So you traced us here?" The captain said.

"I figured the Admiral would be having a resistance party. Was surprised to find you here. And this one." He again pointed to Shax. He grunted!

"Yes! Pray don't stop there prince of darkness. Let's hear what you want of us." Madhav said.

"I want you to assassinate the King!"

A shock-wave ran around the group.

Before anyone could speak, the Admiral said, "And make you the new king. In return you allow us to set up a base here on your planet."

"What makes you think we will believe you? You who plot against your own father." The Captain said in a disgusted voice.

Shax's eyes went red! His nostrils flared and a vein in his temple throbbed, threatening to burst.

"It's not that easy!" Shree said, "Explain them! They'll understand" Shree said holding Shax's hand.

"My father believes, progress must not be sudden! It must be gradual-"

"Come to the point! This is not your regular council." The Captain spat out.

Shax bared his teeth but remained calm. He continued, "He has a plan to execute every city dweller! Every teacher, researcher, writer! Anyone who can think! Anyone who is not essential to the regime will be executed! He promises to bring back the glory days of the Garden of Eden, when the Gods themselves roamed the planet freely."

"And what do you believe in?" Asked Madhav. His tone was conversational, as if these were matters he discussed regularly.

"I believe in progress, Madhav Sharma." Shax said turning his bright eyes to him. He added, "My people suffer through endless hardship and starvation. Slavery, disease, poverty. I want to end it. I want your designs of the steam engine. The engine of change that propelled you out of the dark ages. I want to industrialize my regime. I want to ease the pain of the people. My people! I've seen what your race is capable of. There's nothing to lose if we join hands!" Shax did it perfectly. Not too high, nor too low. Just perfect.

Madhav had to strain to hear what he said. He realised he heard a master at work.

The watery eyes did the rest.

"Then we must assassinate him!" cried the Admiral.

Every head turned towards the one man who knew the schedule of the new King.

"Before the coronation, he'll go to the temple of solace to ask for the blessings of the primeval being. There, he'll be with a six of his loyal guards and my uncle, Beleth. Next in line to pick up where he left. Kill them all and you annihilate the enemy. Leave even one of them and you'll wonder why you ever landed on this planet."

"Why don't we blow up the place?" Shree asked.

"And make him a martyr? No! You must assassinate them. There must be enough confusion among the people about what really happened. You boy! You can circulate conspiracy theories about your uncle. Tell them he wanted to usurp the throne. While we will ascertain people disgust the bloodbath at their revered temple." The Admiral said, throwing a twig into the fire.

"People will be repulsed at the idea of violence inside their sacred temple. This will be a perfect way to sway public opinion against him." Shax said in his unusual wheezy voice.

"Right then! Let's plan the assault." The Admiral commanded.
"I've already done that. We are seen here by my father's spies. While we were having our discussion, my boys were preparing five bodies to look like yours. You'll be declared dead by the next rain. Tomorrow, at first rain, you enter the temple of solace as my slaves. There, we attack!"

The first rain came early. The clouds were dark, and thundered like a storm in store. Madhav woke up earliest and took a stroll by the river where they had camped for a little rest. Shax's men had set up tents which obliterated light entirely. Shax himself had left with Rahab to attend the ceremonial prayers. Before leaving, he had however, shared the helmet of Bor one last time to convince every one of his father's plans. He had left them ceremonial slave robes of black and his wagon drawn by two akki. The white striped bison like animal Madhav had grown fond of.

They dressed and rehearsed their roles one last time.

"Captain you'll be at the altar, with Shax and Shree you'll be right beside his uncle Beleth. Lieutenant Puneet and I will be standing guard at the doorway to the dungeons at the top." The Admiral said.

He drew a map on the ground using sticks.

"Remember, the prayer is over when the King sprinkles water on himself. Everyone will kneel to hide their feet. That's when we strike!" He marked a cross on the map where he had the captain.

"Everyone acts at the same time. Count to three and strike! Captain you take down the King. Shree, Madhav and Lieutenant Puneet engage his guards." The Lieutenant stiffened. "I'll kill the three guards of Beleth!"

"Sounds like a plan!" The captain said in a dim voice. He wasn't too keen to involve in family affairs, as he said it after Shax left. But then, Madhav said, "Sometimes you have to do what's right and not think of the consequences."

They reached the cavern marked with the inverted Y and a circle in its shadow. The symbol of the ancient Kings of Canneti.

They were to wait there until Shax arrived first. He arrived as planned. On the pretext of checking the premises for safety of the new King, left the guards alone at the mouth of the cavern. The captain and the Lieutenant made it look too easy. Years in defence made them kings of stealth.

Next on cue was the Kingsguard. They were to be checked before entering the temple. Shax had, at the last minute, recruited new slaves by citing security concerns. Although the Admiral had advised against it.

"Too many changes in personal guards is always a signal to bolt!", But the prince had gone with it anyway.

The six black robed earthlings waited with bated breath, the arrival of the new King.

"I see a wagon coming through" The Lieutenant said. He had been assigned the lookout duty.

"A what?" Said Shax in an incredulous tone.

"A wagon drawn by two akki"

"There has been a change in schedule!" He said striding forward.

"Someone ratted on us!" The captain yelled.

"No! None of my men would do that. He sensed something. Let me see." Screeched Shax, snatching the spyglass from the Lieutenant.

"Come on! Let's get him." Madhav said.

"He'd enter the city before we even take off." Shree said in dismay.

"No, he won't!" Screamed Madhav freeing an Akki from the wagon and riding it.

Soon, everyone picked up an Akki and rode into the grasslands.

They chased for an hour but couldn't catch him. He escaped and in all certainty, knew about the plot to assassinate him.

The Admiral's lair was a log cabin he made in three hours. The chase two days ago was forgotten and a new plan was being made. Rahab stayed with the crew but Shax came in every fourth rain. His spies told him that the King felt uneasy and changed the plans.

"I don't think it's true. He is planning something and keeping it close to the chest."

"Do you think he knows?" Asked Madhav.

"No. He would have told me! I think he suspects my uncle. I and uncle had a row in his presence over your deaths. Ever since the outburst, he has been silent. What is your progress?"

"I need a few more hours, I mean one rain." Madhav said. He had proposed to use the helmet of Bor to assess the plans of Beelzebub without him wearing one. He used device the apprentice had given him to test. If he could use radio signals as the helmet of Bor, then a well plased radio antenna could sync the King's schema with any helmet he wanted. So far he had managed to transmit signals and make the user unconscious, with a few pops of his thoughts.

Meanwhile, the Admiral made detailed plans of assassinations at the temple of solace, the next time the King decided to visit.

The next day, at the first rain, Shax arrived breathless.

"We must hurry. Father's going into hiding."

"He's the king! He cannot go into hiding!"

"But he is! He has started to build a new castle where he will be approached by no one. No one can meet him, except twice twenty rains."

"That's twice a week." Shree said.

"Yes! In a hall full of men seeking justice, work and all kinds of favours. He has proclaimed himself to be a creature above all. And he refuses to talk to anyone."

"Brilliant strategy! What better way to seal his Kingship, that to proclaim oneself God!" The Admiral said.

"The fort will be ready in four rains. We must strike immediately."

"Your father is a master. I'm sorry he hates the city dwellers. I'd have enjoyed his politics." The Admiral said again.

"Where did you say the castle was built again?"

"The burg of Dalney, North West to the city of Egomyard! It's further down the valley. In the rural."

"Why don't we attack while he moves to the new castle?"

Their plans were made. Preparations complete, rehearsal's done! Eight swords lay in front of the fire they burnt to turn away the cold. The five earthlings, Rahab and two of Shax's men. They picked up the swords and walked up to an akki. The passover was coming and soon the first rain would start.

They rode out in a file, following Rahab who led out of the jungle, into the grasslands.

On reaching the hills, the Lieutenant took out the spyglass he had nicked from the city.

"They are on time. Madhav, be ready."

After waiting for ten minutes, they saw a cloud of dust as the King's caravan passed through the grasslands.

A glint of a mirror reflecting the sun caught his eye. It was the signal he was waiting for!

The Lieutenant yelled, "Madhav, now."

Madhav took out the helmet of Bor and pressing a button, crammed it on his head. Little red and white lights erupted in his eyes. Then they changed into red and blue. He could feel anger! He hated inefficiency. If he could, he'd kill the builder. He had delayed the construction by four rains. These city dwellers got it easy. They thought education made them more privileged than the peasants. They caused his father to die. These educated know-it-alls. He'll show them thir true place, all right. He must calm himself. He was the King, not a commoner. The Caravan should reach before him.

He ordered to slow down the carriage. His Kingsguard slowed down to. He looked out of the wagon and ordered them to slow down Beleth. They would reach after the caravan has reached.

Madhav pulled the helmet out hard.

"It's done! Let's go!"

The wind circled in fierce eddies as the clouds drew closer. Neither the hails, nor the thunder could stop Madhav. He raced through the slope, the akki flying beneath him. The guards grew wary and he could see them move here and there, testing him. Behind, Madhav caught a glimpse of the Admiral covering the other wagon that had Beelzebub. The wagon had the marking of the inverted Y and a circle in its shadow.

With an almighty lurch, Madhav flung himself on the speeding wagon of the brother Beleth. The kamikaze attack shook the akki and snowballed into a crash. With a bang, bits and pieces of wooden carriages flew in all directions. A sharp wooden shrapnel missed the left eye of Madhav as he struggled to his feet. A balloon of dust engulfed them amid the hails and the darkness that came with it.

Behind him, the gang engaged with the others. In front of him, from the upturned wagon, came out Beelzebub. Like a beast, he pounced on Madhav hurling a fury of curses, howling in pain. He was a giant and with each blow he hit, Madhav felt something bleed inside. He coughed a mouthful of blood and tried to reach for his lighting gun. Beelzebub noticed and grabbing it in both of his hands, he flung out of sight. Blood rushed to his ears and he couldn't hear anything. Even the cries of men fighting a foot away drowned. With every ounce of his soul, he asked for help. He flailed his arms in hopes of seizing a weapon, any weapon that could end this. One mighty punch came crashing down his jaw and he felt the world quake. Something brushed against his fingers. Beelzebub had raised his fist again and Madhav knew he won't be able to survive this one. He knew, everything he had done had led him to be here, on this planet, under this beast. It was for him to save this world and its people. And his race with it!

Purple stars shone in his eyes. His fingers fumbled on a wooden shrapnel and pushed it deep into the King's heart, twisting it with all his might.

Blood gushed out of his cruel mouth and his fist froze right above his head. It fell down limp on Madhav's face and his body keeled over. A pool of blood formed in the rain and the dust.

Madhav rose and saw the carnage. Amid the dust he saw the Admiral still fighting one of the aliens looking like the one he had killed. With a sudden roar, this one dived on Madhav and before he could duck, a sharp pain rose through his spine. The Admiral rushed and cut off the alien's head which fell down with a dull thud. Madhav's hairs rose on end and he staggered. He felt discombobulated! Nothing made sense and then everything went dark.

16 EPILOGUE

It had been thirty years since they had first arrived. Shree still felt a tinge of unease whenever she came to the temple of solace. She clutched the hand of her brother Raja and scaled the steep upslope. The memorial of Beelzebub and Madhav's battle was a five minute walk from the craggy hills. King Shax had been adamant that it remain unmarked. The earthlings had moved on, accepted Shax as their King. The Admiral had gone a step further and proclaimed him God, adding "Monarchy can never reign supreme once the people arise".
It turned out to be true. The council re-established within the decade. Democracy had been introduced. Another ship had been built and men were brought in from the refugee colonies of Mars. The earthlings divided in two cultural societies. One that believed the aliens to be Gods and the progenitors of humans on earth – The Ancients. And other that believed in the one true God – The nameless God. Humans intermingled with the aliens and a new breed of demi-aliens were produced. The world was conquered and remained without any boundary, one big nation Canneti, with its capital Madhopur.

THE END

More from the author
An exclusive sneak-peek to
Ankit Roy

THE MONKEY MAN

Epilogue

A starry sky gave way to the predawn darkness and turned magenta like a bruised child. The dim street lights flickering here and there bathed the streets in orange. On the city's eastern outskirts, a heavy darkness fell over the Usmanpur slums. A queasy sense of silence lingered in the air and not a soul stirred.

Delhi slept!

Karna Kumar, assistant police commissioner with the Delhi police squinted at the whimpering kid and climbed out of his blue Mahindra SUV jeep. He could feel the child's agony, the pain and anger very familiar to him. For an instant he was back thirty years, in the filthy shack his father owned, crouching on the floor doused in orange ember glow of the street light in a pool of his mother's blood.

He jerked his head to snap out of the reverie and looked at his mobile phone. It was 4 in the morning. A patrol car or a PCR VAN, as everyone called them was drawn up in the middle blocking the street. The driver spit the red poison he chewed on the dusty wrinkled road and an attentive looking assistant sub inspector threw up his arm that passed for a grim salute. The wireless on his belt crackled with static and a burst of rapid speech issued from it. The dancing lights of the PCR lit up the walls of the shambled building with a faint tick every-time it switched blue to red to blue. A group had gathered round the van staring avidly at the two storied brick walls. Karna slithered through the knot of whispering men to inspect the corpse. A woman's body sprawled on its back, head cocked to the right at an angle that made him raise his hand to his neck. She had a slim, slender body, a red face, mouth agape, a trickle of blood running down its sides. Her eyes were wide open, a tear hovering on its edge. The ASI rushed forward and started jabbering what he had heard. "The family was sleeping on the roof, she went down at 2:30 AM to drink water and when she was at the last step, a person or persons unknown seemingly pushed her down the stairs..."

"Your name, officer?" Karna cut short with his cold voice
without even taking his eyes off the corpse. "Mohammad Noor, Sir"

The ASI was a scrawny lad who evidently spent most of his nights patrolling the streets in his PCR Van investigating everything from domestic violence to lewd comments of incurable boys.

"ASI Noor" Karna said squatting over the dead in his cold unmodulated voice "when did you arrive here?"

"At 3:30 AM. We were patrolling at the other end of the station when the call came. We were here in 20 minutes.

The boy" at this Noor pointed to the child now howling uncontrollably "was with her at the roof. He saw something" Noor turned his head towards the small crowd that had gathered there "something..." he whispered.

"What did he see?" Said Karna more to himself than to the ASI and walked towards the child.

With kindness hard to expect from a 30 year old recluse he hold the boy to his chest and said "Hush boy, it will be all right."

The boy gasped and shuddered twice, then wiped his tears on the back of his hand.

"What did you see child?" he was looking straight into his eyes.

"I saw someone push my mother down the stairs"

It must have been the husband, thought Karna.

It's always the husband. Why the station officer had called him in?

"Who was it?" Asked Karna with a shameful grin.

"I don't know"

"Don't be afraid. No one can hurt you now." he said with a stern look at the husband.

"I don't know"

Karna frowned "Was it a man or a woman?" It could have been the evil mother in law, he thought.

The kid slowly raised his head and looked up at Karna. "A monkey" he said with a gasp.

The kid started sobbing again, tears rolling down his soft cheeks.